Ghumne Chale

Exploration Beneath the Weight of Tradition

PRIYANKA & CHANDAN

Made with ❤ on the Notion Press Platform

www.notionpress.com

Contents

Preface

Ghumne Chale is a story of two worlds: one shaped by the values of middle-class families where hard work and tradition dominate, and another defined by the freedom young people discover when they step away from home in pursuit of education or careers. For many first-generation college students, this new independence comes with an unspoken struggle—the tension between personal desires and the expectations of family and society. In households where love and relationships are rarely openly discussed, young people often find themselves navigating these complexities on their own. Though fictional, the story of Raghuvendra and Shweta reflects the real-life challenges of countless individuals caught between these two conflicting worlds.

The book was born from a moment of uncertainty. After emerging from a difficult past relationship, Raghuvendra proposed the idea of writing to Shweta as a way to make sense of his emotions and the choices ahead of them. It became a way for both of them to stay grounded in the present while contemplating their future. Writing offered clarity, allowing them to approach their journey with mindfulness and reflection.

As they set off on a bus through the rugged landscapes of Nepal, the unfamiliar terrain mirrored their emotional journey. Despite having only met in person once,

Raghuvendra and Shweta had spent nine months getting to know one another from a distance. Their relationship, formed through the complexities of an arranged match, became a delicate balance of tradition and personal discovery. Like many love stories, theirs was filled with both challenges and moments of connection, but their approach was marked by an intentional care to build something real and lasting.

This book doesn't just tell the story of Raghuvendra and Shweta's relationship; it sheds light on the broader generational and societal divides many young people face today. For those who leave behind small towns, cities, or villages to chase their dreams, the freedom to choose a partner feels like a fundamental right. But this freedom often stands in stark contrast to the cultural and familial expectations they grew up with. Raghuvendra, shaped by his experiences across Indian cities and abroad, and Shweta, deeply rooted in her cultural heritage, must navigate the challenges of arranged marriage, family pressures, and the search for authenticity.

Through *Ghumne Chale*, we hope to offer insight to those on similar journeys. This is more than a love story—it's a reflection of the internal and external conflicts that come with bridging two worlds. It speaks to the complexities of love, growth, and the process of reconciling personal freedom with the weight of tradition. We invite you to walk with us through this journey and perhaps find pieces of your own experience reflected in the pages.

— Chandan & Priyanka (02 December 2024)

Acknowledgments

I am deeply thankful to Chandan, whose suggestion to write this story transformed a simple idea into a reality. From the moment he shared it, I was drawn to the thought of creating something that could resonate with so many lives. The journey of writing stretched my limits in the most fulfilling way, and it's your encouragement, Chandan, that made it possible.

To everyone who has contributed to this process, your support has been invaluable. To those who took the time to read early drafts, share insights, and offer thoughtful suggestions—thank you for your generosity. You've played an essential role in shaping this story into what it is today. This has been an unforgettable journey, and I'm grateful to have shared it with all of you.

—Priyanka

This book began as a dream—a dream to write a story that speaks to the hearts of many. When I shared the idea and themes with Priyanka, she embraced it whole-heartedly, without hesitation or need for details. Her trust and enthusiasm made this project come alive.

Acknowledgment

The process of writing was an adventure—filled with moments of excitement, brainstorming, and creative flow, as well as the occasional challenges of missed timelines and maintaining discipline. Priyanka's dedication and belief in this journey kept us grounded, and for that, I am deeply thankful.

—Chandan

We are immensely grateful to Sonal Kumari (NIFT Bhopal, India) for her incredible illustrations that breathed life into the story. A heartfelt thank you to Dr. Akhilesh Verma, Vishesh Mishra, and Saloni Kumari for their meticulous proofreading and invaluable feedback.

To our readers, whose lives and experiences inspired this story—thank you for trusting us with your time. This novel is for you, and your support means everything. It is our hope that it touches your hearts as deeply as creating it has touched ours.

—Priyanka & Chandan

Prologue

As we sat on that rattling bus, winding through Nepal's rugged mountains, I found myself reflecting on the journey that had brought us here. We had only met in person once before, yet we'd spent the last nine months slowly revealing pieces of ourselves online, uncovering not just the intricacies of an arranged match, but the delicate layers of human relationships. Like any love story, ours had its share of ups and downs. But because of our past experiences with love, we were determined to make sure we were ready—truly ready—to accept one another and commit to a future together.

He had crossed continents, flying from Germany to India just to be with me on this trip to Pokhara, a place that would soon be etched in our shared memories forever. Alongside us were his friends Prerna and Akash, adding warmth and familiarity to our journey.

The old bus groaned and jolted along the treacherous mountain road, struggling to grip the uneven terrain—much like us, trying to find our way through the uncharted paths of our budding relationship. A journey that was supposed to last five hours stretched into twelve. But, in truth, our adventure had begun much earlier, back in Delhi, where an eight-hour flight delay foreshadowed the chaos ahead. Tensions ran high at the airport, reaching a peak when a frustrated passenger slapped a staff member.

For a moment, we feared our flight would be cancelled. Thankfully, only the passenger faced consequences, not our journey.

As the bus creaked through hairpin turns, each jolt mirrored my inner thoughts: What if this trip is a disaster? What if we don't connect the way we thought we would? What if one of us gets hurt, physically or emotionally? What if our families find out about our secret plan, and we're judged for it?

Sensing my unease, he gently took my hand. His touch, simple yet steady, calmed my racing thoughts. We exchanged a quiet glance, both acknowledging the shared uncertainty of this adventure—not just the physical journey, but the emotional one we were navigating together. Our fingers intertwined, and in that moment, the bumps on the road felt less daunting.

We talked, our conversation meandering like the road ahead. At one point, he shared a spiritual discussion he'd recently had with a friend in Bangalore, his words carrying a depth I hadn't fully realized before. It struck me then—there was so much more to him than I had imagined.

Our original plan had been to visit the quiet town of Mysore, known for its peaceful surroundings. But I hesitated, thinking it might be too overwhelming. I suggested something simpler, like meeting in **Varanasi**, where I lived. And yet, here we were, on an unplanned adventure in Nepal. The irony wasn't lost on us. The very journey I had been reluctant to embark on had unfolded in the most unexpected way. I couldn't help but smile, realizing that life—and love—has a way of surprising us.

As the bus rumbled on, the scenery changed from lush hills to mist-covered valleys, and I realized that uncertainty is inevitable. I thought back to our first real meeting, away from the safety of our families, at Delhi's Ajmeri Gate train station. The bustling station was a sea of people, the air thick with the chatter of travelers. My heart raced as I searched for him in the crowd, my phone in hand.

"Are you coming from the left?" I asked nervously over the phone.

"No," came the deep voice behind me. "From the right."

I spun around, and there he was—the second time our eyes met in real life, the first being when our families had introduced us back in January. Now it was October, and though we had grown close through online chats, there was still that undeniable excitement—and nervousness—about seeing each other in person again. I couldn't help but burst into laughter.

"Who does something like this?" I asked between giggles.

With a playful grin, he simply replied, "I do."

Our laughter filled the space between us, lightening the moment. In the joy of it all, I forgot the polite greeting I had planned, to join my hands and say "Namaste." Instead, I quickly blurted out the news I had been holding in since boarding the train to Delhi: I had been successful in my interview for a program coordinator position with an NGO focused on education. I learned the good news just hours before our trip.

That moment marked the real beginning of our journey. Just like the unpredictable twists and turns of the bus ride, our relationship unfolded with its own surprises. Yet, as the bus finally made its way to Pokhara, I felt a sense of calm. We had found our way to each other, not through perfect plans, but through embracing the unpredictable beauty of life—and love.

1. Hasty Ties

Something unexpected happening in your life often shows you the reality of life and the power of destiny, any plans do not work other than what destiny has planned for you.

Hi readers,

I am Shweta, and the gentleman you just met is Raghuvendra. Our story begins on a chilly January day in *Varanasi*, a city steeped in history and spirituality. Nestled along the sacred Ganges River, *Varanasi* has been the ultimate pilgrimage destination for Hindus for centuries. With its narrow, winding alleys, the scent of incense in the air, view of delicious street food, and the rhythmic chants from the ghats, the city feels like it exists outside of time.

This is a story of arranged marriage, a practice deeply rooted in Indian tradition, where families invest time, energy, and love in finding the perfect match for their children. It all began with an arranged meeting, orchestrated by our families, whose singular goal was marriage. We met in a modest local hotel room, surrounded by our close family members.

Arranged marriages are often stereotyped as forced arrangements with little room for love or genuine connection. While there is some truth to these perceptions, they don't capture the whole story. Traditionally, arranged marriages were more about two families coming together, leaving the bride and groom to embark on a lifelong journey as virtual strangers. This concept can feel intimidating, even frightening. In the past, young men and women often accepted these alliances without question, conforming to cultural norms.

However, many couples have also felt deeply suffocated, living with partners they never truly accepted or connected with. Thankfully, in recent decades, things have changed for the better. Today, there is much more space for couples to mutually decide upon the partnership even in arranged alliances. However, the dimensions of this space may drastically vary within families and societies. This evolution has brought more balance, giving individuals a voice in shaping their own futures while still honouring the tradition.

We both understood that love alone isn't enough to sustain a relationship, whether arranged or love-based. Along the journey, it takes much more—understanding, forgiveness, growth, learning, and unlearning. There will be arguments, unforeseen challenges, and moments when the very love that once brought two people together feels cornered.

We say this from experience, as we've had our share of love stories that didn't work out. Some may argue that if we are now willing to surrender to an arranged marriage, perhaps it wasn't love at all. But love is complex, and relationships require more than just the initial spark to endure. You'll come to understand the intricacies of our journey as we gradually unfold the layers of our story.

If love alone were enough, the divorce rates in the West would be much lower. The truth is, a lasting partnership requires more than just the spark of romance. Raghuvendra and I both understood these realities, which gave us the strength to be open and mentally prepared for this arrangement. We were not stepping into this lightly, but with the knowledge that a successful story could only be written if we were both willing to commit, adapt, and grow together.

As I sat in that hotel room in *Varanasi*, with my heart racing and my mind a whirlwind of thoughts as I saw the chilled weather outside the window, I was still preparing myself for something that felt like an interview. You see, the concept of arranged marriage had always filled me with anxiety, as if I were surrendering the keys to my own destiny. I had never pictured myself submitting to the notion of an arranged marriage, yet fate seemed to have a different plan in mind. The arranged marriage process is a complex one, where the compatibility of families is a significant factor. Once both families are in agreement, based on the bio-data—a sort of resume detailing job, education, salary, family background, hobbies, and sometimes even astrological details related to the place and time of birth. Both Raghuvendra and I had a look at each other's bio-data and also some pictures shared by our families and said yes for the next step- —an arranged meeting. These meetings are typically organised by an '*Agua*,' a trusted mutual connection who acts as a facilitator between the two families. After a few in-person meetings coordinated by the *Agua*, the bride and groom are finally permitted to meet, usually in the presence of their close families, ensuring the process is respectful and traditional. It's as though one family is marrying another, and the individuals involved, the bride and groom, have the challenging task of building a life together.

It is a ritual steeped in tradition where I (the girl) had to present myself in front of his (*the boy*) family as a way to get the view of *bahu* (daughter-in-law) to be. I was dressed in a *Banarasi yellow saree* (a traditional silk saree from Varanasi, known for its rich fabric, intricate designs, and luxurious gold or silver zari work), adorned with bangles, *Bindi* (a coloured dot or a sticker worn on the centre of the forehead, originally by Hindus, Jains and Buddhists from the Indian subcontinent), and earrings – a complete opposite from my customary wardrobe of western clothing or *kurtis* (short *kurta*, referred to as *kurti*, the attire of females.) with no ornamental accessories to speak of. In fact, when I wasn't venturing outside, I rarely bothered with a thorough face wash or combing my hair. I rarely had any earrings other than studs. This transformation into a traditional, *saree*-clad woman felt alien to me.

The moment arrived, and I was called to the room where our families had gathered. As per custom, I had to touch the feet of every elder from his family to greet them. I performed this ritual, bending awkwardly in my *saree*, before my gaze landed on the person, I assumed was Raghuvendra, he was joining his hands with a quick "Namaste", I continued the process, touching more feet until someone else stopped me. I believe it was the driver. Eventually, I took my seat, glancing around the room to the faces of the people I barely knew.

Raghuvendra, seated directly across from me, came from a village about 60 kilometres from mine and worked as an IT consultant in Germany. After earning his undergraduate degree in IT engineering from Bangalore, he spent a year working in various cities across India. His job allowed him the flexibility to travel and experience life in different places. After just a year of work, he decided to pursue a master's degree in Japan on a fully funded scholarship, where he stayed for nearly six years. Behind him were his elder sister and younger brother. His mother, a retired nurse from Jaunpur district in Uttar Pradesh, sat beside him, while his father, a former high school teacher, sat on a chair facing me. Adding to the lively atmosphere were two children, presumably his sister's, one of whom was playing with her father, who worked as a manager at Bank of America in Delhi. I sat on a chair in front of them, with my family seated behind me, as both Raghuvendra and I were the focus of everyone's attention.

The temperature inside the room was higher than usual due to so many people cramped inside a small space. As the conversation began, our families inquired about our backgrounds, aspirations, and plans for the future. My *bua* (dad's sister) sitting beside me, steering the conversation towards Raghuvendra. She discussed his academic journey, his current job, and his future plans. While they chatted, I couldn't help but wonder about the questions lingering in my mind, such as why he had chosen the path of arranged marriage after his extensive travels, education, and exposure to a multitude of cultures and people. I had even checked out his LinkedIn and Instagram profiles, which suggested he was an extrovert, adventurous, and passionate about physical exercise. I was quite doubtful about whether he embraced this arrangement with an open heart.

I, on the other hand, have been through a long and challenging past relationship, one that had left its mark on my heart. I couldn't help but feel the weight of my past decisions and the promises I had made to my family, to get married after completing my studies. However, I had envisioned a different path for myself, one that allowed my boyfriend time to get settled and to introduce him to my family. It was a plan that held a promise of a future together. Yet, it seemed destiny had its own ideas and plans.

As I reflected on my past, the unpredictability and occasional cruelty of life became evident. It had already taken my dad from me, and now, it had separated me from someone I was deeply in love with. The weight of these losses pressed upon me, and I couldn't find the courage to voice my desires to my family. During my silent struggle, I felt torn between the expectations and promises. It was a moment of internal conflict, and I knew that whatever decision I made would shape the course of my life in ways I haven't thought of. Something unexpected happening in your life often shows you the reality of life and the power of destiny, any plans do not work other than what destiny has planned for you.

Raghuvendra's biodata seemed like a struggle for him to compile—it read more like a professional resume than the traditional marriage biodata. However, it clearly reflected his vast experience, both in his career and his life across different parts of the world. Interestingly, Bangalore emerged as our first common ground outside of societal expectations. I had recently completed my master's there, and it felt like a subtle connection. My uncle reassured me and my mom that Raghuvendra's family had a reputation for being understanding and holding values similar to ours.

Yet, with the weight of my past still heavy on my heart, I found it hard to believe that love could find its way back into my life. I was hesitant to voice my doubts, and the uncertainty left me quiet, unable to express much in that moment.

After the family interview, Raghuvendra and I were sent into a separate room to have our conversation. As we entered the room, Raghuvendra immediately complained about the noise from the construction work happening in the building next door. I agreed and firmly greeted him with a "hello," and shortly after, a man arrived with a kettle of tea and two cups, placing them on the table between us as we settled on the sofa. Raghu poured the tea in both the cups and we chatted coldly while enjoying the hot tea. I had not thought about any questions in my mind. He, on the other hand, seemed ready with a barrage of inquiries about my likes, dislikes, hobbies, and passions. I struggled to recall what I had answered, but I had very few questions to ask in return. My mind was still processing the unexpected turn of events. I hadn't anticipated that we would have to sit down for an extended conversation so soon.

With the day in full swing, we reached lunch hour. Raghuvendra and his family departed to have their meal, while my family set off for some last-minute shopping to select gifts and finalise the marriage. The rush of the day had left me feeling pushed, and I yearned for fresh air other than this. I went outside for some fresh air, despite the biting cold that forced me to immediately go inside the room for warmth.

As the day unfolded, I couldn't help but feel a sense of relief as the proceedings slowed down. When his family called me back for the final conversation, I knew that Raghuvendra had expressed hesitancy about the marriage. Deep down, I whispered a quiet "Thank you," as I had not been prepared for this commitment this soon either. It was a day of unexpected twists, and it seemed that it ended well.

The day ended leaving me with waves of emotions and thoughts. My journey through the complexities of an arranged marriage was far from over, and the future held more surprises and challenges. Yet, in that moment, I couldn't help but feel a glimmer of hope and a sense of relief that we were given the time to truly get to know one another with no rush.

I'm Raghuvendra, my journey has taken me from India to Japan for almost six years and recently, to Germany for my work, all in for my passion of software tools development and user-experience design. This overseas journey had also transformed me from a shy, introverted boy into an extroverted man. However, my journey into this extroversion has been marked by lessons and experiences that I believe has made me more humble, kind and helpful. As my family was somewhat forcing me to embark on this new chapter in my life, I carried with me the hope of forging a connection that would align with my family values. I forced myself to be determined to navigate the path ahead with an open heart, despite the emotional turbulence I was experiencing since the last few months.

I find myself adrift in an ocean of emotions, having recently endured a painful breakup. Calling it a breakup would be a complete lie. We met during a trip in Japan. She is from the northern Indian state, Punjab. It was friendship which blossomed into love. But down the road, we got entangled in a complicated situation where she struggled to make a decisive choice, and I faltered, unable to navigate the chaos with calm. After I moved to Germany, we maintained a faithful relationship despite the distance, staying deeply connected. Yet, as time passed, my parents began pressing me about my marriage plans. They were open to either an arranged or love marriage, but I found myself ensnared in a web of indecision.

To fend off their inquiries, I told them they could continue searching for a potential bride, and if I found her compatible, I would agree to an arranged marriage. Deep down, I suspect my parents knew I had my own plans for my wedding. Eventually, I was introduced to a girl working for an IT company in Chennai. We talked for a week over the phone, but I quickly realised I wasn't emotionally invested. What prompted me to cease communication immediately was her insistence on being allowed to wear hot-pants. Although I agreed in the name of being open-minded and cool, saying she could wear them depending on the time and place. When I asked if she had any other questions related to relationships and life goals, she said no, but then added that she was comfortable living in the city and disliked the mentality of villagers. These remarks turned me off completely. Married life doesn't revolve around clothing and city life; there's so much more to it.

However, this interaction bought me some time to continue working on reviving my relationship with my girlfriend. After months of mental turmoil on both sides, I felt like I was losing my sanity. Eventually, we gave up on each other, recognizing that we were poor communicators, despite being kind-hearted people who never intended to hurt each other. I am profoundly grateful to my friends who, with unwavering patience, listened to my tangled emotions. They offered suggestions they believed might help, never casting judgement on me or her. I can't even count the number of times I burdened them with my troubles, yet their support remained a beacon of solace during my darkest hours. Despite the separation, my heart clung to the love I had for her. Seeking a fresh start and some much-needed peace, I returned to India with a mission in mind: to spend quality time with my parents and give them a well-deserved break.

My parents had dedicated their entire lives to ensuring that my siblings and I had everything we needed. They worked tirelessly and sacrificed their own wishes to make ends meet, provide us with the best education, and support our dreams. Now, it was my turn to express my gratitude. I decided to plan a trip to Ujjain, not only to give my parents a well-deserved break but also to distance myself from the emotional baggage I had been carrying. I was determined not to let them down and to make every effort to make them feel loved.

I love travelling and have always wanted to show my parents different places. Every time I think back to our last trip together to Sri Lanka and Japan, I feel a deep sense of pride. With my savings from my first job in India, I was able to fund the entire trip for my mom, dad, and myself. I had only just started earning, but knowing my parents were getting older and less comfortable with long journeys, I decided not to delay the experience. It felt important to share those moments with them while we still could. Their happiness was beyond words. My uncle-aunt, as well as my sister and brother-in-law, also joined us on the trip. I found myself as the bachelor trip guide for three of these couples. It was such a memorable experience, witnessing their revived love for each other. Taking time away from the daily routine can sometimes rekindle love and gratitude that may have been forgotten. This trip provided just that, a beautiful reminder of the enduring bonds we share.

After returning home from the Ujjain trip, I was informed that a prospective bride's uncle wanted to meet me. Casually, I asked for more pictures of her and agreed to the meeting. I received more photos of her and sent mine to her uncle. Honestly, I couldn't see any beauty in her. When you're blinded by sorrow and unresolved emotions, it's difficult to see anything even in bright sunlight.

The day arrived, and her uncle came with his younger brother and two other people who were mutual family connections, *Agua*. Following tradition, we prepared the nicest snacks, food, and sweets for them. My dad engaged in conversations with the guests, while my mom was alone in the kitchen with a lot of work, so I took control and fully immersed myself in cooking, cleaning, and serving the guests. They asked me about my life and salary, which is the ironic part of arranged marriages. The bride's family often expects a well-settled and high-earning groom for their daughter without caring much for compatibility and education level.

Dowry, though frowned upon in society, is a result of the bride's family trying to secure a well-earning man for their daughters by offering a lot of money. There is a need to treat and educate girls in the same way boys are. If this were the norm, a boy's family wouldn't ask for dowry, and a girl's family wouldn't try to buy the most suitable match with money. Fortunately, my family is not part of this dowry loop. All they wanted was an educated girl with social and family values.

At the end of the day, I took a step into the unknown, agreeing to meet the girl my family had chosen for me.

My family believed that her education and background from a reputable school in *Varanasi*, and the university from Bangalore, suggested she is intellectually compatible with me. Also, coming from a humble family background, she possessed qualities such as adaptability and strong family values.

Meeting Shweta was a unique experience for me, primarily because it marked the first time, I had met a girl with the consent and arrangement of two families. It was also interesting to learn that she also studied in Bangalore. Unlike most of my female friends, who are independent, outspoken, and often wear their hearts on their sleeves, Shweta appeared to be a different kind of person. What struck me the most was her silence and the absence of any questions or concerns. It left me wondering if she was under pressure from her family and I couldn't help but feel a sense of confusion and uncertainty. The fact that the arrangement of the meeting was organised just a day before I had a flight to Delhi, from where I was to fly to Germany, was unsettling. They even wanted to conduct a *Roka* ceremony, a ritual promising that the families would not seek any other partners for their child. This rushed approach raised significant doubts in my mind. Why was the girl's family in such a hurry? Was there something wrong with the girl? Was she being coerced because she didn't have a dad? These questions lingered, adding to my uncertainty about the situation.

I expressed my concerns to my dad, stating that I couldn't proceed with this marriage plan. It seemed absurd to me that while we take our time analysing products before purchasing, marriage is being treated as a quick business transaction. My dad proposed to her family that we let the two of us discuss and understand each other. If we liked each other, we could proceed with the wedding; if not, there was no point in forcing the marriage. I hoped I could reach out to her and have a candid conversation to clarify our thoughts and feelings. I believed that having a one-on-one conversation with her would help us avoid making any hasty or misguided decisions. This seemed like a reasonable step to ensure clarity and mutual understanding. I was determined not to end up making any stupid decision in my desperation to get rid of pain and uncertainty from my complicated mental state.

As the day drew to a close, there was still doubt in the air and no clear answer had emerged. The path ahead remained uncertain, and the weight of our family's expectations lingered in the backdrop of our thoughts. I returned back to Germany hoping I had managed to avoid getting hitched. However, little did I know, it was only the beginning of a new chapter in my life. A few days later, I received a message from Shweta's mom, who wanted to share Shweta's mobile number so we could interact. Initially, she was a bit reluctant to share her contact information; I suppose it's a custom in small villages where a girl's parents often view sharing contact details unfavourably until both families agree on the wedding. My dad confirmed the validity of my assumption.

2. The Humble Hi!

Isn't it fascinating how our culture, history, and religion offer us comfort through specific days throughout the year, with some being especially sacred or significant.

"Hi! Shweta"

The message beeped on my WhatsApp chat, catching my attention. The number displayed was unfamiliar, starting with (+49). It was Raghuvendra. His message was both surprising and expected. My mom had hinted to me about sharing my number with him, urging secrecy in our communications. So, when Raghuvendra's DP flashed on my screen, I greeted him with a warm,

"Hello! Raghuvendra," saving his contact as "Raghuvendra" feeling a curious sense of anticipation.

It was **January 26ᵗʰ**, a day that held dual significance for us: Republic Day and *Saraswati Puja* (a Hindu festival dedicated to the goddess of wisdom, music, arts and education, Saraswati). Our conversation naturally turned towards reminiscing about our childhood celebrations. As we exchanged memories of patriotic fervour and the vibrant festivities of Saraswati Puja, we delved deeper into the ways we used to worship Goddess Saraswati.

We recalled our childhood belief in the deep influence of Saraswati *Maa* (mother) on our lives. It was no surprise to learn that we both used to keep peacock feathers with chalk powder between the pages of our notebooks, believing that the feathers would bring us wisdom and good marks. Raghuvendra shared fragments of his childhood, portraying himself as a spirited yet dedicated student. In contrast I, speaking to him as a complete stranger, recounted my experiences as an average student, preferring to remain inconspicuous in the classroom shadows. I also mentioned how I used to skip some classes and wander around *Sarnath* (a small town on the outskirts of the city Varanasi). It's dotted with Buddhist temples, archaeological parks, and a charming little museum. *Sarnath* felt like a peaceful escape from the boring classes and city's noise.

As we continued talking, the looming spectres of arranged marriage and family expectations weighed heavily on my mind throughout our conversation. Along with that, my mind wandered to the uncertainty surrounding my career. For months, I had been considering relocating to Delhi, the capital of India, to prepare for the Banking Officers exam after completing my master's degree. Even though I had finished my studies, I was still in Bangalore, unsure of the next steps.

Compounding my internal turmoil was the realisation that I was talking to someone my family had already marked as a potential match for me. This knowledge weighed heavily on my mind, leading me to limit our interactions to just casual chats or brief voice calls. Each exchange was tinged with a sense of apprehension, as I navigated the delicate balance between familial expectations and my own aspirations for the future.

Just a few days into our conversations over calls and chats, our family started asking about a final decision—either a clear "yes" or "no". It was such a short span of time to conclude anything. Although we didn't learn much about each other, we felt comfortable talking to each other. Uncertain about each other's feelings, strengths, or weaknesses, we ultimately decided to say "yes" to each other and to our families on **January 31st**. While Raghuvendra was not very happy about this approach of our family, I was quite aware of this and accepted it as natural; it didn't seem strange to me.

With the decision made, the planning for the *Roka* ceremony commenced. It was agreed that my family would visit his family on **February 14th** and his family would come to us on **February 18th**. Coincidentally, the latter date held immense significance, as it fell on the holy day of *Shivaratri* (the day when God Shiva and Goddess Parvati were married). Reflecting on this, it struck me that the beginning of our journey together was unknowingly spiritual in nature. And even the day I received his first text message was auspicious. Isn't it fascinating how our culture, history, and religion offer us comfort through specific days throughout the year, with some being especially sacred or significant. This might also hold true for people from other cultures and religions, or even for those who believe in lucky days or numbers.

I had to go shopping for the *Roka* ceremony, which was planned suddenly. It was my first-time shopping for such an event and that too at a new place where I had just recently moved, Delhi. It made me a little overwhelmed. I had heard that it takes a lot of time to buy a *saree* and jewellery, but I decided to keep things simple and my whole shopping was done in an hour. I was childishly excited about wearing a beautiful saree and looking like my mom's wedding picture with all the glamour of traditional jewellery and props. It felt like I was about to live out the experience of being the doll I used to dress up as a bride when I was a kid.

I went to a local shop in Purani Delhi and bought a *Banarasi saree* worth ₹3500. It was cream coloured with a red border and came with a matching red blouse piece. I gave the blouse to a tailor, hoping to get it stitched on time. Additionally, I bought a *Chunari* (a special bridal *dupatta,* a long shawl-like scarf traditionally worn by women in India) and some faux jewellery, which included a red necklace, a *maang tikka* (forehead ornament for females), matching earrings, and bangles—a mix of metallic *kangan* (a kind of bangle broader than usual *churis* (a kind of thin colourful glass bangles worn by females in India and its neighbouring countries) for the wrist worn by women). When the day arrived on the **18th of February**, fully cladded in Indian traditional attire, I looked at myself in the mirror, I could hardly recognize my reflection. I looked so different, almost transformed into a woman from a girl. At that moment, I realised how much a girl changes, not just in appearance but in essence, when she becomes an adult and enters a new phase of life. I shared pictures of the ceremony and myself in the *saree* and other items with Raghuvendra.

Raghuvendra:

After the *Roka* ceremony, Shweta sent me pictures of the event. I saw her and the happy faces of our family members. Shweta looked truly beautiful in the pictures. Indian girls, I believe, look the most beautiful in their traditional attire. I'm not trying to be sexist here; it's genuinely what I feel. To me, the *saree* isn't just clothing; it embodies emotions, culture, and a familial vibe. For a moment, I even imagined that if she became my wife, she would look stunning in that kind of *saree*. However, these thoughts were fleeting as my mind was consumed by overthinking about my relationship with my girlfriend. Images of her wearing a *saree* flashed before my eyes, and

I found myself in a state of emotional turmoil. I couldn't understand what was going on inside my head.

Shweta:

As weeks drifted by like leaves on a gentle stream, our connection started to build with each passing conversation. We approached one another cautiously, revealing fragments of our lives with a measured touch, mindful not to expose too much too soon. From the initial exchanges of text messages, we slowly traversed the terrain of voice calls, then tentatively dipped our toes into the waters of sporadic video chats.

Despite the geographical expanse that separated us and the occasional silences that punctuated our communication, our bond flourished. I was quite accustomed to short-hand texting, with most of my sentences trailing off with too many dots, which often left him confused and unimpressed with my communication style. He effortlessly coaxed me away from the shorthand that had become second nature to me. His keen insight into my texting habits, particularly the trailing dots at the end of each message, caught me off guard. "Your texting behaviour reveals that you're an overthinker," he remarked, his words a mirror reflecting a facet of myself I hadn't fully acknowledged.

How had Raghuvendra discerned my inclination for overthinking with such accuracy? It was a question that lingered in my mind, mingling with a sense of awe and curiosity. Yet, his observation struck a chord within me, resonating with a truth I had been overlooking since years. With quiet resolve, I embraced this aspect of myself, silently committing to a journey of growth and self-improvement.

Meanwhile, I was deeply focused on preparing for the Banking Officer exam. Amidst the intense study routine, our conversations became a source of comfort and companionship, offering relief in my solitary pursuit of knowledge. Each chat, whether brief or deep, kept us connected despite the distance and the challenges of our individual paths.

What drew me closer to Raghuvendra were his career aspirations and his profound passion for his work as a software consultant. His kindness and shared values, such as reverence for the elderly, familial bonds, and a minimalist lifestyle, resonated deeply with me. While I found solace in religious practices, he pursued a path of spirituality, enriching our conversations with diverse perspectives. His insights into health and dietary habits, though challenging to adopt at first, left a lasting impression. Despite the initial struggle, I integrated some of his advice into my daily routine, recognizing the value they brought to my well-being. In our journey of mutual discovery, amidst the backdrop of academic pursuits and personal growth, our connection blossomed, anchored in shared values and a mutual desire for growth and understanding.

It was the first week of **April** when Raghuvendra's first gifts arrived, a thoughtful assortment of earrings, lipstick, and *kajal* (a black cosmetic used around the eyes in South Asia). They marked a significant milestone in our budding relationship, serving as tangible tokens of his affection and perhaps hinting at a shared future that I had already begun to envision. Despite occasional irregularities in his communication patterns—late replies and sporadic texting—I chose to overlook these discrepancies, attributing them to the intricate dynamics of our arranged marriage setup, differences in our time-zones and the weight of professional work.

However, what struck a painful chord was Raghuvendra's apparent oversight on my birthday, the **27th of May**. While his gifts—a collection of novels, a *Kurti*, and chocolates—were undoubtedly thoughtful, they lacked the emotional resonance I had yearned for. For me, it wasn't the material aspect that mattered most, but rather his emotional presence and acknowledgment of the significance of the day. The absence of such recognition left a lingering ache in my heart, a silent plea for deeper understanding and connection in our evolving relationship.

In the aftermath of this disappointment, I grappled with conflicting emotions, torn between my desire for emotional connection and the societal norms dictating our relationship dynamics. Despite the hurt, I found myself clinging to the hope that our bond would deepen over time, transcending mere material exchanges to embrace a deeper, more meaningful connection built on understanding and emotional availability. After he explained his absence, I realised I had expected too much from our arranged marriage. He wished me a happy birthday over text message and did not call me for the next 24 hours. It made me think maybe expecting love was too big. So, I decided to lower my expectations to avoid more disappointment.

Raghuvendra:

It's true that I wasn't fully emotionally available, as I was still caught up in the past. But I also knew that moving forward was the best thing I could do. She mentioned her birthday well in advance, so I knew she wanted me to be part of it. I ordered novels because I knew she loves reading, chocolates because they seemed like a safe bet—something most girls enjoy according to the movies—and lipstick to show my affection. I made sure to text her exactly at midnight to wish her, but I got caught up with work. I was scheduled to attend an important business meeting at my office at the same time, so I couldn't call her. I think things got more complicated because we were in different time zones. Later in the evening, I felt emotionally weak, thinking about my ex and the celebrations we used to have together. I just couldn't find the strength to call or text Shweta. Then, one of her friends messaged me on Instagram, explaining how hurt she was, and made me promise not to disclose her name. Then I came to know I had hurt her, and I thought she deserved an explanation. Everyone deserves that—it's how human relationships work. So, I texted her, trying to explain, but she was so annoyed that her replies came off as slightly rude. I felt the coldness, so I called and explained that I had been busy. But that wasn't the whole truth. The complete truth was, 'I was busy, and when I was finally free, I was emotionally unavailable for her.

Though I'd consented to the arranged match with Shweta, my inner world was in disarray. Thoughts of my ex persisted, her name echoing in conversations with our mutual friends. The bond I shared with her elder sister only heightened my empathy as I witnessed their family's struggles with their autistic sibling. Their brother, with his endearing nature and extraordinary artistic talent, stirred a profound connection within me.

Yet, it was their father's journey towards acceptance that resonated deepest. It took him years to view his son's condition not as a curse, but as a behavioural disorder—a transition laden with emotional weight. Meanwhile, my ex grappled with anxiety and the pressures of her final year master's studies alongside the turmoil at home. Despite my deep concern, our communication faltered amidst the chaos. I failed to articulate my feelings, presuming she couldn't prioritise our relationship amid her familial and academic obligations.

The burden she bore only intensified with her elder sister's unmarried status. Despite her elder sister's insistence on proceeding with our relationship without concern for their father's reaction, my ex found herself in an emotionally vulnerable state, unable to reach a definitive decision. Reflecting on our past, I recognize my error in assuming and not communicating openly. It's a lesson etched in hardship, a reminder that assumptions only serve to widen the chasm between people.

After months of mental turmoil, I began to question whether I truly loved my girlfriend or if I was simply a kind soul who fell for anyone in need of love. Similar thoughts echoed in my budding relationship with Shweta. What if the friendliness and sporadic connection I felt toward her came from a place of compassion and an understanding of the struggles she and her mother faced without her father? The doubt gnawed at me, especially after agreeing to marry her. The idea of telling her that I neither had any feelings for her nor any attraction filled me with a profound sense of guilt. Deep down, I wished all relationships could just vanish from my life for a while.

It's strange how our mind overthinks, amplifying our fears until they manifest as extreme emotions—pain, loss, uncertainty. I was caught in this whirlwind of thoughts, unable to see the simple truth: if I could silence the noise, I'd realise I always had the choice to pick any path. But instead, I found myself waking up in the dead of night, drenched in sweat, haunted by nightmares and anxiety attacks.

When it happened for the third time, I decided enough was enough. Something had to change. Around the same time, a friend reached out to me, struggling with his own mental health due to personal and professional issues. He was having suicidal thoughts, feeling utterly helpless. Hearing his plight made me pause and reassess my own situation. In my case, I wasn't suicidal, and none of the people involved in my tangled emotions were at risk of dying if things fell apart. At least, that's what I told myself at the time.

Shifting my attention from my own mess, I threw myself into helping him. I listened to his struggles, reminding him that his existence mattered, both to his loved ones and the world. I urged him, over and over, to consult a psychologist or a counsellor and to inform his workplace about what he was going through. Within a few weeks, he got the help he needed from his company and managed to overcome those dark thoughts. Watching him recover was a relief, but it also brought the focus back to my own life.

I realised something then—I was always the cheerful, optimistic one, eager to help others see the best in themselves. And yet, here I was, feeling utterly helpless in my own situation. Why hadn't I thought to consult a psychologist? That question lingered in my mind. It felt like a turning point.

I made an appointment with a psychologist and poured out my struggles to her. I could sense her concern as she listened—it wasn't just about my relationships, but my lack of clarity in work, my dwindling motivation, societal expectations that seemed to weigh me down, and everything else. She suggested an extensive course of in-person therapy sessions. It was a wake-up call. But ironically, I never showed up for the in-person therapy sessions.

That moment became a personal resolution: I would not lose myself in loving or hating anyone. Instead, I began taking small steps, cutting away the clutter, and giving direction to the endless conversations I had with myself. Slowly, I started to find my way.

I cut myself off from my mutual friends with my ex on social media; many of them still don't know. To those who stayed in touch, I made it clear not to mention her during our conversations. One thing I appreciate about my ex and myself is that after our final goodbye, we never contacted each other again, respecting the bond we once shared. During our final conversations, when she learned about Shweta and the early demise of her dad, she was very empathetic. Being a strong believer in *karma* (the force generated by a person's actions in Hinduism and Buddhism, believed to determine future life experiences), she wished me happiness and said she didn't want to bring bad *karma* upon herself by taking away Shweta's share of my love. When we were together, there was always a lingering fear deep within us, a fear that one day we might find ourselves in a situation where we would have to part ways gracefully, as a tribute to the beautiful moments we shared. And now, that situation has arrived. It was a poignant reminder of the power of our thoughts—the power to shape and manifest our reality. Although it marked the end of our relationship, I felt a sense of relief and emptiness altogether. That day, I realised what it means to let someone go if you love them. It's tough but sometimes love is not enough, there are situations, and life takes twists and turns. You realise, your best efforts in the moment were not best enough.

But a few weeks after final conversations with my ex, I experienced an unexpected emotional event that shook me deeply. Again, I was in a miserable emotional state, missing her while knowing it was time to move on. I felt helpless, very angry with myself and the situation. One day, I confided in a friend about my situation, seeking advice on how to navigate my feelings for Shweta. Her words struck a chord within me: if I didn't love her, I should let her go, as someone else might cherish her. The weight of her advice hit me hard. Though I had hoped to focus on building a new chapter with Shweta, the shock of the realisation was too much to bear.

I knew I had to be honest with Shweta about my uncertainties. Despite knowing it would hurt her; I couldn't enter a relationship where my heart wasn't fully committed. There was no point in prolonging a conversation filled with insincerity. With a heavy heart, I shared my doubts and suggested we inform our families about my hesitation. Although confused and saddened, she agreed.

Shweta:

On **June 16th**, Raghuvendra called me and told me he still had feelings for his ex and was unsure about marrying me. I was hurt deeply. **June 16th** was already a painful day for me, as it marked the day of my dad's passing away. I had gone to the temple that morning, seeking solace and strength. He said he needed space and wanted to meet me in person to talk things over. I felt a mix of emotions—sadness for my family, who had hoped for our union, and a profound sense of personal hurt.

It showed me once again that I didn't need anyone to be happy. Reflecting on how my ex had cheated on me, I couldn't help but draw parallels with my current situation with Raghuvendra. Although Raghuvendra and I weren't deeply involved yet, I had developed feelings for him and had started to imagine a future together. However, the unresolved issues and the emotional turmoil we were both experiencing made it difficult to envision a stable relationship.

Given my past experiences, I realised that my insecurities and fears were resurfacing, making me question the foundation of any potential relationship with Raghuvendra. Despite the initial connection and shared moments, I felt it was crucial to protect myself from getting hurt again. The best solution I could think of was to control my feelings and take a step back. This decision was not easy. Yet, I knew that continuing without addressing our emotional baggage and uncertainties would only lead to more pain. I needed to focus on my own stability and goals, ensuring that I could make independent and wise choices for my future. Though, there was a strange sense of relief that he was honest, but also a deeper longing to understand more about his past. My curiosity got the better of me, and I found myself scrolling through his Instagram posts, piecing together the fragments of his previous relationship. I discovered her name, and they had shared many pictures together. I also discovered that Raghuvendra and his ex were no longer following each other on their personal Instagram accounts. However, they still followed each other through a shared Instagram page. It suggested that Raghuvendra might not be completely over her. This realisation made it clear to me that I couldn't envision a future together if love was absent. I knew I deserved a relationship filled with genuine affection and commitment, especially when I was ready to offer the same in return.

I confided this to one of my close friends, sharing what I had discovered. She mocked the coincidence, saying, "Your ex cheated on you with a girl with the same name. There must be some unresolved issue in a past life with that name." Her humour lightened my mood, making me feel a bit more at ease. With her support, I finally decided to shift my focus back to myself and my own well-being.

That night, unable to bear the uncertainty any longer and driven by her advice, I decided it was time to confront the situation directly. I texted Raghuvendra: "Something feels off. I don't think we can truly connect with this unresolved tension between us. If we are not 100% sure about this relationship, what's the point in continuing? Let's end it here, inform our families, and go our separate ways."

Raghuvendra responded thoughtfully, "Thank you for being honest, Shweta. I understand. This isn't easy for me either. There's an invisible boundary between us, and it's only going to grow wider if we continue like this. I agree with you—let's stop now to avoid any further emotional hurt and inform our families.

3. Post Confession

However, I now realise it was unfair to expect someone else to fix my issues when they were grappling with their own.

As days passed, we didn't exchange any texts after the last conversation we had. During all this, I felt incredibly isolated. I chose not to discuss it with any friends, as it involved family matters, which only made the situation more difficult. I believed it was Raghuvendra's responsibility to talk to his family before I involved mine. But, neither of us dared to bring this news to our family.

Throughout this challenging period, I came to realise how profoundly our childhood experiences shape us. I recognized my long-standing need for love and connection, a longing that emerged after losing my father. As a child, I dreamt of marrying a man who would love and care for both me and my mother—a responsible partner who could provide the stability and affection I craved. This longing for security and belonging influenced my decision to end my previous relationship when I couldn't find the sense of responsibility I needed in him. The uncertainty in my relationship with Raghuvendra triggered these deeply rooted fears, making it even more difficult to handle. I expected a stable and dependable partner in Raghuvendra, especially since I was already struggling with my own emotions. However, I now realise it was unfair to expect someone else to fix my issues when they were grappling with their own.

Even though I had asked Raghuvendra to end the relationship, and he expressed a similar desire to inform our families, the prolonged silence where neither of us communicated this to our families was stealing my peace of mind. Around this time, I even began discussing the possibility of breaking off the engagement with my younger cousins, weighing the potential outcomes. I vividly recall being on a group video call with them, posing the question, *"Who do you think will be the most shocked if we call off the wedding?"* They unanimously replied, *"The whole family."* I laughed it off mockingly, but deep down, my heart sank at the thought of hurting everyone involved. The weight of their expectations made the decision even harder to bear.

But as the suffocation continued, I realised that I needed to make a change. To start, I decided to find a place where I could live independently and establish a source of income, even if it meant beginning with something small. After moving into a small, rented apartment, I started tutoring a child. This not only gave me a sense of purpose but also provided me with my first source of income. The money I was making wasn't much, but many young people who rely fully on their families for financial support can relate to the joy of feeling like a lesser burden. It was a step in the right direction—a move toward reclaiming my sense of self-worth and financial independence. I embarked on a journey to reclaim my happiness, determined to build a life I could be proud of, one small step at a time. Alongside this, I prepared for my bank officer exam and also for an interview for the position of Program Coordinator at an NGO working in the field of rural literacy. Establishing a proper routine became essential, as it helped me balance both my physical and mental well-being. My day started with meditation, followed by a workout session. After a hearty breakfast, I would head to the library, often skipping lunch, and later went out for tea in the evening. Usually by 8 PM, I would return to my room, have dinner, and end the day with a peaceful one-hour walk on the terrace. Slowly but surely, I felt myself growing stronger, embracing each day with renewed purpose.

Two months Later

By dedicating myself to a consistent routine, I began to appreciate the mental peace and personal growth I had achieved. Although I felt lonely and vulnerable during the first few weeks in Delhi, living apart from my old friends amidst emotional turmoil, I soon recognized the power of being with myself. Initially, the deep sense of loneliness was overwhelming, but through my intentional small actions, it transformed into a journey of self-discovery and growth.

One day, out of the blue, I received a call from Raghuvendra's sister, who said she and their mother were in the city for a few days and wanted to meet me. I was completely taken aback by the sudden call. I considered asking Raghuvendra to help me prepare for what might come out of my meeting with his sister and mom, but it felt awkward to text him after nearly two months of silence. My overthinking only added to my unease. It's funny how a communication gap can transform a budding relationship into strangers. Despite everything, I still held a glimmer of hope in my mind that this relationship could work. After hours of internal struggle, I finally managed to text him. His response came quickly, but it was casual and disappointing. He simply said, "You can go if you want to." I asked him if he had mentioned our uncertainty about marriage to his family, but he denied it, saying he was still planning to talk to them. Trying to console me, he said, "You should go and enjoy your time with them without overthinking it. But if you feel even a pinch of doubt, just drop the plan, and I'll handle the rest." His words reflected his own emotional struggle, and I began to feel empathy for him.

I dressed myself in a light pink *Chikankari kurta* (a garment featuring chikankari, a traditional embroidery style from Lucknow, India) with white *kari* work and paired it with round metallic earrings he had gifted me, adding a touch of kajal, a bindi, and a small pendant. I completed the look with golden strap sandals. I booked a cab and headed to the restaurant where we planned to meet. As I arrived at the gate, I quickly checked myself in the mirror and entered the restaurant. The gatekeeper opened the door, and the cool air inside immediately calmed me. As I stepped in, I found myself lost in the words of the song *Main Phir Bhi Tumko Chahunga* playing in restaurant: "*Kal mujhse mohabbat ho na ho, Kal mujhko ijazat ho na ho, Toote dil ke tukde lekar, Tere darr pe hi reh jaunga.*" (Which means: "Tomorrow, I may not have your love, Tomorrow, I may not have your permission, but with the pieces of my broken heart, I will remain at your doorstep.")

The lyrics seemed to echo my own emotions to some extent, grounding me in the present moment. I snapped out of my thoughts when I saw his sister approaching me with a big smile. As I walked toward the table, I noticed that Raghuvendra's sister was seated with her husband, their mother, father, and—much to my relief—my own mother, who had come all the way to Delhi to meet his family. She believed that it would help build a stronger bond between our families. My mom has always dreamt of me being part of a loving and caring family. She often said, "I want you to have all the love you may have missed while growing up in absence of your father."

Sitting beside his sister, I glanced at my mother. Looking back, I realise how much extra weight she must have carried on her shoulders after my father passed away. She never wanted me to feel the absence of a dad, and I never felt like I was missing out compared to my friends. But even so, there were moments when I felt lost for words whenever my friends talked about their fathers. I especially missed my dad during my parent-teacher meetings, when my mom had to attend alone.

What a strong, caring woman she is—my role model. I want to be just like her.

My mom quickly started a conversation with his mother, and they continued talking as if they had known each other for years. Meanwhile, I found myself lost in thought, imagining how they would react when they eventually learned that we were planning to call off the marriage. The thought of it made me feel suffocated, even in the cool, air-conditioned restaurant.

Soon, the waiter arrived with our orders. We finished the meal, but I could barely focus, my heart aching with the weight of the situation. Unable to endure it any longer, I subtly signalled to my mom that it was time to leave, mentioning that it was getting late. Sensing something was off, she understood, and, after a while, we bid everyone goodbye and left the restaurant.

On the way back, my mom noticed the unease in me and asked gently, "Is everything all right?" At that moment, I knew I had to confess everything to her. I laid out all the confusion and uncertainty that had been building between Raghuvendra and me, though I didn't mention that we hadn't been talking for months. My mom listened carefully and then offered reassurance, suggesting that things would settle with time. "It's just the emotional waves affecting you both right now," she said, trying to comfort me. But her words only deepened my worry. Could I truly find happiness in this? What if we ended up getting married under family pressure? Would our families ever fully understand our emotional struggles?

I began to question everything. Could I really find the love I had always craved for in my partner? Do couples in an arranged marriage ever fall in love with each other? After all, once the wedding is over, families tend to step back, leaving the couple to navigate their relationship on their own. And how could we ensure our happiness if genuine love was missing? These thoughts kept swirling in my mind, weighing heavily on my heart and leaving me even more uncertain about the future.

After I dropped my mom at the station, I couldn't help but notice the tension lingering on her face and the slight glimmer of tears in her eyes. I tried to comfort her, telling her not to worry and assuring her that I would be fine and happy. Reluctantly, she left with a little more ease.

When I returned to my hostel, I had dinner and then wandered up to the terrace, listening to loud music, trying to clear my mind. That's when I received a text from Raghuvendra: *"How was the meeting?"* I replied that everything went fine and shared the conversation I had with my mom. He seemed just as worried, admitting that he was anxious too since he hadn't spoken to his parents yet. The weight of our unspoken concerns hung heavily between us, deepening the sense of uncertainty we both felt.

Raghuvendra then shared that his consultant in Germany was nearing completion, and he needed to find a new workplace. This uncertainty left him emotionally unstable. For some reason, our conversations restarted after this event. I noticed a shift in my perspective; Raghuvendra's struggle and my own ambitions intertwined in a way that made our relationship feel more real and less idealised. We both faced challenges, and sharing these experiences brought us closer together. It wasn't a fairy-tale romance, but a genuine connection forged through understanding and support. I felt that we all look for a great friendship quality in our partners, we were exactly doing that by sharing our struggles be it personal or professional.

The interview date was approaching closer, and my revived interactions with Raghuvendra provided a peace to my anxious mind. As I prepared for my interview, I noticed how Raghuvendra was deeply involved in helping me. He offered valuable tips on making myself more presentable in front of the interviewers, emphasising that they knew nothing about me and that it was up to me to present myself effectively. Using his Google search-driven insights into the program coordinator role for an NGO working in the education sector, he really helped me narrow down the study materials for the interview. His guidance and encouragement made a significant difference in my confidence levels.

One evening, during a discussion about his future career plans, Raghuvendra asked me where he should join his consultant position. I advised him to choose the place where he could see the brightest future for himself. In response, he casually mentioned, "Wherever I join, you'll have to join me." I had a big 'Yes' to say but no words came out. I was already in love with his honesty, helpful nature and kindness. But I had to protect myself from being emotionally hurt, so I just casually said, "hmmm".

After he accepted the offer to join his new job in Sweden, he mentioned, 'Oh! Look, it seems your dream of moving to a cold place has come true.' I felt a sense of shyness but could only smile at his response. Above all, I was happy to notice he still remembers my likes and dislikes. I easily sweat out and in summer it gets horrible. So once during our initial conversation, I told him that I love cold places because I could be relieved from my sweat.

Our casual exchange made me feel more at ease with Raghuvendra. Despite the earlier uncertainties and challenges, his involvement in my life and his shuttle comments about our future together gave me a sense of comfort and reassurance.

As we navigated our respective challenges, I found myself rooting for him. At the same time, I remained steadfast in my commitment to my career goals. This period of our relationship, though fraught with uncertainty, was also marked by a deepening bond and a shared understanding of the importance of personal and emotional stability.

Raghuvendra:

Just a day after I confessed my uncertainties, as I reflected on my connection with Shweta, I realised that while marriage with her might not be in my heart, I truly valued the happiness and companionship our conversations brought. Respecting her suggestion to break ties, I understood what she must have been going through. Continuing our conversation in such an emotional state felt wrong, so I agreed. Shweta was wise enough to recognize her own feelings, and I needed clarity as well. During the two months we didn't speak, I immersed myself in work, though I knew I should eventually share this with my family. Yet, the fear of their reaction held me back.

Two months later, my sister mentioned that our mom planned a trip to Delhi for some work and was hoping to meet Shweta and her mother again, away from the traditional expectations. I wasn't sure if Shweta would agree, given everything, but I trusted she wouldn't hurt anyone. Just as I was contemplating this, Shweta messaged, asking if there was any update about the upcoming meeting. She was also uncertain about attending. My casual reply, "Whatever you want," felt too indifferent. So, trying to comfort her, I encouraged her not to overthink and to enjoy the time. After the meeting, both my mom and sister were impressed by Shweta's genuine nature and that of her mother, and I felt a deep appreciation for Shweta, knowing she didn't let the turmoil show.

That night, I texted Shweta, asking about her experience. She shared the conversation she had with her mom, and a wave of guilt washed over me, knowing the emotional strain my indecision must have caused. Over those two months, I found myself reflecting on Shweta and the calmness she brought, which allowed me to confront my own feelings. Gradually, I recognized that my love for my ex had faded naturally, and I was beginning to feel drawn toward Shweta.

One Sunday, sitting in my backyard and watching the birds, I drifted through my memories with Shweta. I felt a sense of purpose, almost as though a guiding force had placed me on a path to love and care for someone who needed it just as much as I did. She loved me, and I had developed a genuine sense of love and appreciation for her in return.

For the first time in two months, I felt a sense of happiness after talking with Shweta, partly because she understood my internal struggles and unknowingly supported me through them. As the days went by, our conversations grew longer, from simple text exchanges to video calls. With time, my feelings for Shweta deepened, and I sensed she felt similarly. There are moments when the philosophies and ethics we hold are tested in profound ways, and this journey with Shweta has been one of those moments for me.

Shweta studied diligently for her Bank Officer exam. I watched her pore over notes, revise with almost religious fervour, and frequent the library as if it was her second home. She did everything within her power to succeed, yet despite her best efforts, she didn't pass. I couldn't help but feel a twinge of disappointment, thinking that perhaps if she had started studying earlier or planned more meticulously, the outcome might have been different. But then, I shook off my judgmental thoughts and considered the turbulent emotions she must have been grappling with.

When we first started talking, I often asked her what she was passionate about. Her answers were always vague. Over time, however, I discovered that she was an avid reader. Even amidst her rigorous exam preparation, she found solace in books. This realisation brought me a certain comfort; I sensed that her failure was just a step in her journey of self-discovery, a journey she was not fully conscious of herself.

Around the same time, I was e-mentoring school children through an NGO and had assigned them a writing exercise: "Where do you see yourself in the next ten years?" It was meant to stretch their imagination and hone their writing skills. Curious, I posed the same question to Shweta. Her response astounded me. She envisioned a life marked by humility, self-growth, and the presence of a supportive partner. This was a revelation; I saw in her not just a writer, but a person who deeply valued relationships. Here is the original writing work from her:

"Me After 10 Years

The first rays of sunlight poured through my window, lighting up my room. Another day had dawned, bringing with it new hopes and aspirations. The chorus of melodic birdsong drifted in, and the fresh, cool, and crisp air patted my face, trying to wake me up. Yes, it was a perfect morning for me.

Good morning! I am Shweta, a 37-year-old woman. I run an NGO for elderly people and a school for orphans. I have always dreamed of doing some good for the elderly. I have a special affection for them, and I believe every emotion in us is tied to something from our past. For me, it stems from a personal loss. I lost my father when I was just six years old, at such an age one is too young to fully understand life. Me and my mom were not prepared for such a profound loss. Losing him was incredibly hard for us but leaving us must have been even harder for him. He died in a tragic road accident. I still have an unanswered question for God "Why me?"

Lost in thought, I suddenly felt a warm hug from behind, calming me. "Good morning, Baby" my husband whispered in my ear, bringing me back to the present. Then the bell rang. Oh! It was time for our workout. We woke up, got fresh, and went to the field. At our NGO, the day starts with morning exercise guided by trainers for each group of people.

People had already gathered and were ready for the workout, which I believe is one of the best ways to start the day. Shaping the most precious gift given to us by God—our bodies—is the best way to value it. After an hour of workout, the routine continues with fieldwork in the garden. The gardener advises people on how to improve the plants in their assigned plots. Afterward, breakfast is served, prepared with products from our farm, which are fresh and free of toxic chemicals. A group of people work here as cooks and prepare nutritious food.

The school is managed by a few teachers and a group from the NGO oversees its administration. Our NGO not only helps people but also provides employment. We welcome ideas for the betterment of the NGO. People here can pursue their hobbies, helping them feel satisfied and find inner peace. We couldn't have found a better location for such a positive organisation than this peaceful place, far away from the city's rush and the relentless pursuit of jobs that often sidelines passion and hobbies.

After breakfast, I return to my work, which I mostly do from home. Managing an NGO and a school is challenging, but I try to give my best. The happiness and blessings of the people are the best rewards I receive every day, keeping me motivated. True success is having peace and a smile on your face at the end of the day, and I experience this every day.

Being an iconoclast in life was not easy—it was more like sailing your boat against the waves. But doing something different and good for society, beyond a regular job, has always been my dream. I am blessed to have a supportive partner and a caring family who backed me in this decision.

Of course, starting something like this requires good planning and financial stability. But as the saying goes, "where there is a will, there is a way". I waited for an opportunity because the universe always provides what you desire; you just need to grab it. That happened to me too. I had the opportunity, and I seized it.

In the beginning, my job was prime focus, and the NGO was secondary. But now, the NGO is primary, and my job is secondary. I believe that whatever you do should have a purpose that not only motivates you but also gives you inner peace, driving you to work harder. We get one life, and it's our choice whether to lead a lavish life on the same track or to do something different for society.

Ten years ago, life was a chaotic struggle as I searched for where I belonged and who I was meant to be. What would my future be? What was in my destiny? Would I have a peaceful life? Each person I met had their own fascinating story, which made me wonder about mine. I never wanted to be confined within the box of life that only included myself, my partner, my kids, and my personal world. Often, ideas came to me through observation. Living this long, with its ups and downs, life teaches us many things. The best we can do is to make ourselves stronger and learn from every mistake. My belief and trust in God have increased over time, and I hope they continue to grow in the future."

In our regular conversations, Shweta often mentioned her love for teaching, an activity that brought her joy. This, coupled with her passion for writing, made me confident that whatever path she chose, she would find happiness in a role that involved either writing or teaching. Despite her preparations for banking exams and interview for a program coordinator position for an NGO, it was clear to me that her primary goal was financial independence. She was ready to take any job to achieve that.

It's easy to perceive someone's life as normal from the outside, but we often only see the tip of the iceberg. I was fortunate to glimpse beneath the surface and understand Shweta's true struggles and aspirations. I remember helping her practice for her interviews, playing the role of a tough and exacting teacher. My intentions were always to push her towards excellence, to see her succeed.

In those moments, I realised the depth of her resilience and the clarity of her ambitions. Shweta was on a path of self-discovery, and though it was fraught with challenges, I had no doubt that she would find her way. Her journey was not just about passing an exam/interview; it was about understanding herself and her true passions. And in that, she was already succeeding. I don't know when, but I found myself introducing Shweta as my future wife to my friends in Germany. A friend once teased me, "how is your Sweetu?". Instantly, I fell in love with that name, and that's how she got her nickname.

4. **The Interview**

*The magic of travelling together lies in how it unveils the
true colours of those who embark on the journey.*

26th August

This day marked a significant milestone in my life—
my very first job interview. Unlike my master's thesis
viva, where I was surrounded by the comfort of familiar
faces, this experience was entirely different. I stepped into
an unknown environment, filled with a sense of
excitement and anticipation. This wasn't just any
interview; it was for a position with an NGO, a job I had
aspired to for a long time. Honestly speaking, I always
hoped for a meaningful job, but desperation for financial
independence made me confused about my life goals. But,

when I got selected for the interview round, I started to get a sense of direction and a closer reflection at my goals. In the moment, I realised the opportunity to work for a cause that aligned with my values felt like the next big step toward fulfilling my career dreams.

I had prepared diligently for this interview, dedicating countless hours to case studies, revisions, and sharpening my skills. The competition was intense, with many candidates possessing more experience than I did. Despite moments of self-doubt, I was determined to give it my all. This opportunity meant more to me than just a job—it was a chance to prove my capabilities and take a meaningful step toward my goal of independence.

The preparation process itself became a journey of personal growth. It pushed me to become more organised and disciplined, not just in my studies, but in every aspect of my life. I developed a routine that balanced study, exercise, and mindfulness, all of which helped me build confidence and resilience. In many ways, this preparation was as much about proving to myself what I was capable of as it was about landing the job.

I dressed professionally in a pink salwar paired with white leggings and a white *dupatta* (a long shawl-like scarf traditionally worn by women in India). I wore light reddish pink lipstick and *kajal*, complemented by small shiny studs and flats with golden straps. As I sat on the worn wooden bench outside the interview room, my nerves started to gnaw at me. A girl emerged just before my turn; her face drawn with frustration. She muttered something about irrelevant questions, her voice heavy with disappointment. In that moment, my manageable anxiety spiralled into a tidal wave of dread. Fear surged through me, overwhelming any sense of calm I had left.

In an attempt to calm myself, I remembered Lord Krishna and quietly chanted,

"Hare Krishna, Hare Krishna,

Krishna Krishna, Hare Hare,

Hare Rama, Hare Rama,

Rama Rama, Hare Hare."

When my name was called, I walked into the interview room where four elderly men were seated around a table. They motioned for me to sit on the empty chair facing them and asked to make myself comfortable.

The first question in my interview was about my inspiration for joining this NGO. I paused briefly, gathering my thoughts, and then answered confidently. I mentioned that my inspiration was Mother Teresa, and, as fate would have it, it was her birthday that day. One of the interviewers raised an eyebrow and cross-questioned me, "Oh, she seems to be the inspiration for many, including one of the Miss Worlds." I took a deep breath and responded with a smile, "Yes, Priyanka Chopra."

That set off a barrage of questions, focusing deeply on my understanding of the role of a Program Coordinator. I managed to answer most of them, though I stumbled a bit on a few. Once the case study and technical questions were over, one of the interviewers asked about my hobbies. I mentioned my love for reading novels, and how I'm an avid reader. I also added that I had read Priyanka Chopra's memoir, **Unfinished.** As a follow-up, I clarified the earlier question: while Mother Teresa wasn't exactly Priyanka Chopra's inspiration, she was someone Priyanka admired. During her Miss World interview, Priyanka had been asked who she thought was the most successful living woman, to which she answered, "Mother Teresa." The spoiler, of course, was that Mother Teresa had passed away in 1997, and the interview took place in 2000.

The conversation flowed easily after that. I mentioned that I also love to write poetry and stories. Intrigued, one of the interviewers asked me to start a story based on an imaginary scenario. I asked for a moment to gather my thoughts and began, though I stopped midway. He smiled and encouraged me, saying, "I believe you can do it." His kind words gave me confidence.

When I mentioned that I graduated in 2022, the interviewer seemed a bit surprised. He complimented me, remarking that I had performed impressively for a fresher. This acknowledgment gave me a quiet sense of pride. He then asked how I would adapt to the work environment, and I confidently responded, assuring him that I am a quick learner and trust my ability to handle challenges wisely. Though I didn't feel my answer was particularly remarkable, the interviewers seemed pleased. Their encouraging words left me with a wave of optimism as I walked out of the room, unable to contain the unstoppable smile that spread across my face.

It's truly amazing how hobbies can unexpectedly support us in our professional careers, even though I wasn't fully aware of how my personal interests might come into play. I worked really hard to achieve everything I planned, but it wasn't until recently that I realised just how beneficial my love for reading novels has been. Hours spent engrossed in books have helped me develop the focus and discipline necessary for the intense study required in my career.

I honestly can't remember how reading became such a central part of my life, but I do recall being addicted to comics as a child. Then, as a teenager, romantic novels captured my heart and became my go-to escape. Now, I find myself open to reading anything—from self-help books to spiritual guides.

As the interview concluded, an overwhelming sense of relief washed over me, as if a huge weight had been lifted off my shoulders. That morning, I had called Raghuvendra for some final words of encouragement. Instead of the usual "good luck," he simply said, "Do your best." When I later told him how it went, he was genuinely glad to hear that I had done exactly that.

As days passed, my conversations with Raghuvendra became more frequent and meaningful, deepening our bond in ways I hadn't anticipated. I found myself more mentally available and positive, which was also reflected in how I connected with Raghuvendra. Finally, the day came when Raghuvendra told me he was planning a trip to India to meet me. We both longed to meet in person, and the excitement was mutual. While our phone conversations had given me a rough idea of his personality, meeting face-to-face felt crucial for a relationship that could potentially last a lifetime.

Raghuvendra had spent almost six months in Mysore during his undergraduate studies for an internship and found it to be a perfect place for two people to spend time together. Mysore offers a balanced mix of city life and calming natural sites, with good transportation services and easy access through buses, trains, and private cars. He also planned to visit his friends in Bangalore, the biggest city nearby and home to the international airport, before meeting me. Since Bangalore is only about 150 kilometres from Mysore, he had already booked his flight tickets to Bangalore, and planned to spend 4-5 days with me if I agreed.

However, the idea of travelling so far from Delhi for a secret trip made me uneasy. It was also an issue of safety and security as there are many instances of date crimes. I was not afraid of the extremes, as I could get a good vibe from him and was already an admirer of his honesty. But still, confusion cluttered my mind. I sought advice from my close friend Ritu, who had been a comforting presence since childhood. Ritu is like a protector for me, a more guardian-like friend whom I can trust. She advised me to keep up the pretence of an arranged marriage and to be cautious with my plans. Given Raghuvendra's emotionally unstable behaviour, which I had shared with her, she advised that meeting in Delhi would be a safer and more practical option. I agreed with her reasoning and proposed this to Raghuvendra.

To my immense respect for him, Raghuvendra didn't hesitate to cancel his original plan just because of my insecurities. This gesture meant a lot to me. I'm someone who doesn't easily venture out with unknown people; I cherish the comfort of my own group. Raghuvendra's willingness to adapt reassured me of his kindness and understanding. However, he believed that travelling together would reveal all sides of each other and is one of the best ways to truly learn about one another. So, instead of giving up, he came up with a plan that made me feel more at ease.

Raghuvendra spoke to one of his friends, Prerna, who he knew from his master's days in Japan, and Akash, Prerna's husband from Gorakhpur, India, and expressed his desire to explore Nepal with them. Prerna is from Nepal, so definitely it was a great idea to have a local friend as our tour guide. And they were happy to include me in the trip. The idea of going to Nepal made me feel more comfortable, knowing it wasn't too far from Delhi and that the presence of another girl added an extra layer of emotional security for me.

Despite the whirlwind of emotions—excitement, anxiety, and anticipation—about travelling with three strangers, I decided that this trip would be the ultimate test of the patience and effort I had invested over the past months. We created a WhatsApp group named "GHUMNE CHALE (or, *Ghum-ne Ch(a)-lay*, which literally meant let's go travelling)" which included Raghuvendra, Akash, Prerna, and me.

Prerna lives in Raipur with her husband, who is a professor at Kalingam University, Raipur. Their presence brought a sense of familiarity and safety to the trip. I had never travelled by flight, so I was a bit uncomfortable booking the tickets myself. They booked our flight tickets from Delhi to Nepal, and little did I know that the fun of the trip would begin with those tickets themselves. My tickets were humorously booked under the name "Mr. Shweta Kumar," a clerical error by Nepal Airlines that mistakenly labelled me as a male.

As the trip drew closer, our bond deepened, and our excitement grew. We even started shopping together, albeit virtually, suggesting clothes and accessories to each other. Raghuvendra recommended a pair of sandals, and I eagerly planned my outfits for each day of the trip, meticulously writing down my plans on paper. I remember the courier boy recognizing me due to the daily arrival of parcels for 3-4 days straight.

In a gesture of care, I ordered a *Panchmukhi* (five headed) *Hanuman ji* (the Hindu monkey god of wisdom and power) idol for Raghuvendra, mindful of his bike accident a few months back. *Hanuman ji* symbolises strength and protection from mishaps, and I wanted him to feel protected and empowered.

This trip was more than just a meeting; it was a leap of faith. It was about stepping out of my comfort zone, confronting my insecurities, and giving this budding relationship the chance it deserved. I was ready to embrace whatever the journey held, trusting that every step I took was leading me toward a future that, despite its uncertainties, held the promise of something beautiful and meaningful.

Raghuvendra:

My perception of (for) Shweta changed irrevocably when she agreed to travel to Nepal. Until that moment, I harboured lingering doubts about her capacity to make independent decisions. She had always seemed to move in the shadows of her family's expectations, her choices largely influenced by their guidance. But her decision to step outside her comfort zone and embrace the uncertainty of a new journey altered my view entirely. Shweta stood up for herself and seized the chance to embark on this journey, showing a side of her I hadn't fully appreciated before.

In a conservative Indian family environment, where parental guidance is held in high regard and deviating from it can result in harsh judgement, asserting one's individuality is no small feat. The fear of being labelled a troublemaker or a burden often prevents young people from expressing themselves fully. But Indian parents need to realise that controlling a grown child isn't the answer. Instead, it's essential to instil strong values and lead by example. With this foundation, children can develop better judgement and grow into wise, civic-minded individuals.

Ironically, despite their best intentions, many parents remain unaware of the troubling behaviours some children engage in behind their backs. From multiple sexual partners to drug and alcohol abuse, smoking addiction, and sometimes even criminal activity, these hidden realities often go unnoticed. The gap between what parents believe and what actually happens is painful to acknowledge. When parents eventually come to learn about these incidents, it's easy to understand their fear of their children going off track.

During my undergraduate years, I witnessed many of my batchmates turn to heavy drinking and smoking, initially driven by the desire to look "cool." Some girls exchanged sexual favours for gifts, switching boyfriends based on convenience and benefits. At the same time, many boys were also used, abused, and in some cases, exploited their girlfriends. Relationships became a status symbol, with sex seen as the ultimate goal. Looking back now, I realise how hollow and meaningless most of those relationships were, revolving around superficial displays, sex, and temporary benefits. The depth and sincerity that should form the core of any bond were often missing.

The concept of this trip with Shweta wasn't just a spontaneous idea; it was rooted in the tapestry of my own experiences. I reflected on my journey, which had taken me from the bustling streets of the cities (Varanasi, Bangalore, Ranchi, Kota, Mysore, and Delhi) in India where I had spent quite some time, to a six-year sojourn in Japan, followed by almost two years in the Germany. Each place has contributed to the shaping of my worldview, illustrating the profound impact that exposure to diverse cultures and ideologies can have on one's mindset.

Growing up in a small village in Varanasi, the contrast between my humble beginnings and the broader world was stark. Through my travels and interactions with various cultures and intellects, I came to understand the relativity of reality. People often conform to societal norms without questioning them, a realisation that has fundamentally shifted my perspective. Seeing Shweta take this leap of faith was not just about the journey itself but about the broader, personal growth we both were embracing.

The magic of travelling together lies in how it unveils the true colours of those who embark on the journey. Having traversed many landscapes and cultures, I've observed how different people reveal their authentic selves when set against the backdrop of new experiences and unfamiliar places.

Some travellers, their spirits alight with the thrill of exploration, transform into vibrant raconteurs. They are the ones who fill the air with their animated stories and insights, each tale a thread weaving into the collective narrative. Their energy is contagious, infusing every interaction with a sense of wonder and enthusiasm that makes the journey feel exhilarating.

In contrast, others seek refuge in quietude, finding peace in the moments between destinations. Their silence is not mere absence of sound but a deep, introspective calm. It speaks volumes about their inner world, offering a glimpse into a more contemplative side of the human experience.

Then there are those whose hearts are open and hands ever ready to assist. Their presence is a steady beacon of kindness, illuminating the path for others and providing a sense of comfort amid the trials of travel. Their support is often the glue that holds the group together, making the challenges seem less daunting.

However, the journey also reveals those who lean towards inertia, content to let others take the lead. Their reluctance to contribute can cast a pall over the group's collective spirit, turning what should be an adventure into a test of patience.

Some individuals are easily unsettled by the unpredictability of travel. Their frustration with every hiccup is palpable, their tolerance for inconvenience thin. Their responses can sometimes disrupt the group's harmony, revealing how quickly their patience can wear thin.

Stubbornness, too, makes an appearance, as some dig in their heels and refuse to compromise. Their rigidity can become a barrier, obstructing the smooth flow of the journey and creating discord within the group.

Yet, amidst the myriad personalities, there are those who radiate warmth and camaraderie. Their presence is a source of joy, their friendliness is a balm for weary travellers. They have an innate ability to turn even the most mundane moments into cherished memories.

Nevertheless, one may encounter those who are overly cautious with their finances, reluctant to part with a penny more than necessary. Their frugality can sometimes introduce friction, contrasting sharply with the spirit of shared adventure.

Travelling together thus paints a rich, multifaceted picture of human behaviour. Each person adds their own unique hue to the journey, and it is through these varied interactions that the essence of true companionship is revealed. Every trip becomes a canvas, reflecting the intricate fabric of human nature and the bonds formed in the crucible of shared experiences.

Travelling together indeed serves as a revealing mirror, reflecting the diverse facets of our personalities. Dwelling on my experience, I thought of travelling together with Shweta as a way to know more about her. And also reveal me to her. Consequently, I devised a plan to persuade Shweta to meet me in person, recognizing the importance of assessing our compatibility in a practical scenario. Initially, I suggested travelling to Bangalore or Mysore, eager to immerse ourselves in a new environment where we could explore each other's personalities more deeply. Shweta seemed amenable to the idea until she discussed it with her friend Ritu, who cautioned against it due to societal conventions and potential repercussions if things didn't work out.

Acknowledging Shweta's concerns, I respected her apprehensions but couldn't shake the desire to meet face-to-face. Thus, I proposed meeting in Delhi, where she felt comfortable. At least, this is what I felt. However, the travel aspect remained unresolved until a serendipitous conversation with my friend Prerna from Nepal, who resided in Raipur with her husband, Akash.

Inspired by a spontaneous impulse, I reached out to Prerna, expressing my intention to visit Nepal with a prospective partner. To my delight, she embraced the idea wholeheartedly, eager to join us on the journey. With Prerna's enthusiastic support, I proposed the trip to Nepal to Shweta, who finally agreed.

With the trip now in motion, I sensed a glimmer of excitement mingled with apprehension. Yet, I remained confident in Prerna's ability to discern Shweta's compatibility with my personality, given our long-standing friendship. As we discussed logistics, I offered my assistance in obtaining Shweta's passport, symbolising our mutual commitment to confronting the challenges and uncertainties that lay ahead.

Ultimately, Shweta's decision to embark on this journey signified a moment of empowerment, a testament to her courage in breaking free from familial/societal expectations. Together, we embraced the unknown, prepared to navigate the challenges and forge our own path forward, guided by the shared desire to explore the depths of our connection.

As I kept interacting with Shweta, marriage and love emerged as profound points of contemplation. The prevalence of failed unions across different societies lingered in my mind, each shaped by unique cultural norms, unresolved personal issues, childhood traumas, and familial expectations. In developed nations like America and Germany, love marriages are common, yet divorce rates are high. In contrast, India maintains a tradition of arranged marriages, often with lower divorce rates. Yet, drawing conclusions about happiness in marriage based on these patterns would be premature. Both societies have their share of happy and toxic marriages.

I have come to firmly believe that love can blossom in both arranged and unarranged unions, provided both parties are willing to invest in and understand the depth of their commitment. However, reality often diverges from this ideal. In conventional arranged marriages, families sometimes rush the process and withhold important information, while couples may be reluctant to disclose past relationships. This secrecy can lead to emotional turmoil and ill-preparedness for marriage, creating fertile ground for extramarital affairs.

On the other hand, love marriages can struggle with the blurred lines between lust and love. As time reveals deeper layers of personality and challenges such as financial strain and parental responsibilities emerge, the foundation of mutual respect and compromise may erode, leading to marital breakdowns. Despite the unique challenges faced by both types of marriages, neither guarantees success. What is crucial is an open dialogue between partners, exploring their values, habits, and life aspirations. I question whether parents are ready to impart such wisdom to their children before they encounter marital discord.

These reflections left me unsettled, yet I remained committed to the sanctity of marriage. I sought a partner who could be both a companion and a lover, someone with whom I could share life's joys and trials. While nothing in life is guaranteed, I was determined to actively shape my destiny, embracing both victories and defeats with grace. For me, the journey toward a fulfilling marriage began with the recognition of the importance of informed decision-making and taking ownership of my choices.

5. Flight to Nepal

My heart was full of anticipation and a sense of new beginnings.

Finally, the day came when Raghuvendra was back in India, and we were in the same time zone. Our good mornings aligned, as did our good nights. He was in Bangalore for two days, catching up with his old friends. This trip was a secret; his family had no idea he was in the country. I, on the other hand, had informed my mother about him coming to India and meeting me, though I didn't share any details about our trip to Pokhara. It felt like keeping a delicate balance - being open enough to share yet holding back just enough to keep this journey between us, free from external opinions and expectations.

The day before Raghuvendra was set to arrive in Delhi from Bangalore, I had completed my packing, ensuring I had all my usual clothes, shoes, a few beauty essentials, some medicines, a gift for him, and some chocolates. I feel like calling him Raghu, instead of Raghuvendra, definitely I had developed deep affection for him. I could barely sleep with the thought of meeting Raghu after everything we had been through. As I lay in bed, memories of our two-month silence flooded my mind— how distant we had become, and yet, when we restarted our conversations, the joy it brought to both of us was undeniable. It was like reconnecting with a part of myself I had missed. The excitement and nervousness about seeing him again the next day kept me wide awake, my heart racing with anticipation.

I knew he was just as eager to meet me. I could sense it in the tone of his messages, especially when he texted me at 3 a.m. right before catching his flight from Bangalore, "Coming to you soon, baby girl," he wrote.

His words made my heart skip a beat, and I couldn't help but smile. It was such a simple message, but it was filled with the warmth and excitement we both shared for this long-awaited moment.

It was around 7 AM when I found myself sitting at Indira Gandhi Terminal 3, near the exit gate, my heart pounding in anticipation. I scanned every possible exit, trying to catch sight of him. With my phone in hand, I called him and asked a simple question, "Are you coming from the left?"

But his response wasn't on the phone—it was right behind me. His deep, manly voice, rich with warmth and gravitas, filled the air. "No," he said, "from the right."

I turned, and there he was. Our eyes met for the second time in person after nine long months of virtual interactions. We had spent hours talking, sharing, and connecting online, but now, standing face to face, it felt surreal. He looked effortlessly casual in a t-shirt and blue jeans and a long jacket, walking toward me with that familiar ease.

His embrace was warm and grounding, pulling me into the reality of the moment. My heart raced with excitement and nervousness. Unable to contain myself, I burst into laughter, the tension melting away.

"Who does this?" I asked between giggles, amused by the surprise.

With a twinkle in his eye and that playful grin I had come to adore, he simply replied, "I."

It was such a small exchange, yet it captured the essence of us—our journey, our connection, and the comfort we found in each other's company.

Our laughter filled the air as we stood there, two people who had taken a leap of faith to meet in person. Moving ahead, I forgot the greeting I had decided, joining the hand and saying "NAMASTE" which I did after a while. The morning began with a sense of anticipation as I booked a cab and headed back to my place with Raghu. Once we arrived, I quickly made a cup of coffee for him while he freshened up. The warmth of the coffee seemed to comfort him, and he relaxed, his tiredness evident after the long journey. Just two hours later, Akash and Prerna joined us. It was my first time meeting all three of them together, and while I was a bit nervous, Raghu seemed at ease with Prerna, joking and laughing reminiscing about old days in Japan. I didn't want to stop the conversation, so instead of preparing some breakfast, I ordered aloo parathas for everyone, and we shared a hearty breakfast.

As the day unfolded, Raghu started to feel unwell, exhausted from his travels. He lay down on my bed and fell asleep, while Prerna and I prepared lunch together. It was a simple, peaceful moment, bonding over the preparation of food while Akash was occupied with an online class on the balcony.

After some time, I went to check on Raghu. He was awake, looking a bit better but still worn out. I offered him a glass of water, which he accepted with a quiet "thank you." Then he asked, almost hesitantly, if I could give him a head massage as his headache was bothering him. His request was genuine, and I could see how much the journey had taken a toll on him. I agreed, and as I gently massaged his head, I could feel the tension leaving his body. He relaxed visibly, and for a few moments, we simply enjoyed the calm.

Just as we were settling into the tranquillity of the moment, my phone rang. It was the NGO I had given an interview to, informing me that I had qualified for the interview. A surge of happiness filled me, and I couldn't contain myself. I started jumping with joy and, in a burst of excitement, hugged Raghu without thinking. He smiled warmly at me, understanding how much this meant. After I calmed down, Raghu reminded me about the parcel he had sent earlier, instructing me not to open it until he was with me. I handed it to him, my curiosity piqued. He asked me to close my eyes, and when I opened them, I saw the beautiful gift he had brought—a delicate blue butterfly pendant with brown lace and matching earrings. It was stunning, and I could feel the thoughtfulness behind it. It symbolised so much more than just a gift—it was a mark of our growing bond.

In return, I gave him my surprise—a Lord Hanuman idol, with the Hanuman Chalisa (prayer) handwritten by me tucked inside. I suggested he read it daily for strength and protection. The appreciation in his eyes melted my heart, and in that moment, we exchanged a look that spoke volumes. We hugged, a quiet but powerful gesture, conveying emotions that didn't need words.

After lunch, we went for a nap, trying to gather energy for our upcoming trip to Nepal. Our flight was scheduled for 4 PM on the same day, and we were filled with anticipation. However, upon arriving at Indira Gandhi International Airport, we discovered that our flight was delayed by four hours and would now depart at 8 PM. Later, it was postponed again to 2 AM. The frustration of waiting began to set in.

As we navigated the expansive airport, my emotions were all over the place. Despite the situation, I kept thinking about Raghuvendra who was sitting beside me and chatting. Lost in my thoughts, I realised he was the man who had been a constant presence in my life from the last 9 months, the one who had brought me joy and sorrow, and had helped me grow. He was also the one my family had chosen for me. And now that I have started to accept him as my own choice, these thoughts made my heart swell with a mix of gratitude, love, and apprehension.

As we walked around, Prerna and Raghu shared some of their memories, their laughter echoing through the terminal. I was acutely aware of my actions and words, often retreating into silence, lost in my thoughts and emotions. I felt a complex mix of love, uncertainty, and hope for the future.

Finally, when it seemed like the waiting would never end, a man erupted in anger, slapping a Nepal Airlines staff member and blaming them for the delay. The chaos and noise around us only added to our exhaustion and frustration. I felt a surge of anxiety as the crowd gathered the tension palpable in the air.

But eventually, the moment we had been waiting for arrived after ten long hours. The flight arrived and a wave of relief washed over all of us. As we settled into our seats and prepared for take-off, I felt a surge of gratitude and affection for Raghuvendra. His support and understanding made me feel safe and cared for, reinforcing the deep connection we shared. Raghuvendra introduced me to the flight details since it was my first time on a plane. He is the one who convinced me to obtain my passport long before this trip was even planned. From the moment we arrived at the airport, he had been guiding me through each step of the process, from check-in to security checks, to finding our gate. It was really nice of him to do this so patiently, without making me feel awkward or inexperienced. Despite the delays and the emotional rollercoaster of the day, his presence turned a potentially stressful situation into a memorable and comforting journey. His thoughtful explanations and calm demeanour helped ease my nervousness, making the whole experience much more enjoyable and less intimidating.

Despite the long and frustrating wait for our flight to take off from New Delhi airport, I was excited for the adventures that awaited us as I heard, "Welcome to Nepal". My heart was full of anticipation and a sense of new beginnings.

That is how we spent day 1 of togetherness away from the watchful eyes of our family and against the etiquette of conventional arranged marriage.

6. The Bumpy Ride

The bus creaked and groaned as it navigated the hairpin turns, while my thoughts mirrored the journey.

As we arrived in Kathmandu, we were greeted by the crisp, cool air that reminded me of winter. I only had a light cotton kurti on, but the chill was a refreshing change from the heat back in Delhi. This was my first time travelling outside of India. We reached Kathmandu around 3 AM, and I noticed a familiar scene of cab drivers rushing toward passengers as we exited the airport, just like in India.

We quickly hailed a cab and headed to our hotel, eager to settle in after the long journey. However, upon checking in, we were informed that our reserved room was unavailable. The manager, trying to make amends, offered us a spacious room with three beds instead. Prerna and Akash took the other room, while I found myself sharing the room with Raghuvendra.

Despite the long wait at the Delhi airport and glitch in our travel plan, there was an undeniable peace in finally being here. While the excitement of exploring a new city made us ignore our bad travel experience, our exhaustion made us quickly succumb to a deep sleep, each of us dreaming of the adventures that awaited us in Kathmandu the next day. The cosy cold night of the city, combined with our travel fatigue, made for a peaceful night's rest, setting the stage for a memorable exploration ahead.

The next morning alarm rang from an incoming call from Prerna's phone, jolting me awake. As I woozily opened my eyes, I saw Raghuvendra sleeping soundly in the bed next to mine, looking as peaceful as a baby. The soft morning light was streaming through the windows, filling the room with a gentle glow. It was time to get ready, as Prerna and Akash were already up.

I quickly got out of bed and decided on my outfit for the day: a white loose crop shirt with black polka dots, paired with black pants. I added a touch of makeup—just my usual routine of moisturising cream mixed with *Gulab-jal* (Rose water) and a swipe of dark brown lipstick. I felt pretty good about my look. Raghuvendra, on the other hand, was dressed casually yet stylishly in a mustard yellow short kurta and white pants.

Being the last one to get ready, I hurried as everyone patiently waited by the door. Just as I was about to step out, Raghuvendra suggested with a playful smile, "Earrings *pehen lijea, Mohtarma*"; which translates to "wear the earrings, O lady".

I couldn't help but blush. Raghuvendra had bought me a pair of beautiful blue earrings, and his gentle reminder made me feel special. I quickly put them on, completing my look. With everyone ready, we stepped out of the hotel, excited to explore the wonders of Kathmandu. The day promised new adventures and experiences, and I couldn't wait to see what lay ahead.

Prerna's brother joined us too. Interestingly, he was the reason Prerna and Akash had met through Raghuvendra. Prerna and Raghuvendra had been friends since their days in Japan. When Prerna's brother, Ramesh developed a declining vision condition, she sought Raghuvendra's help to find medical contacts in India. Raghuvendra, ever resourceful, connected her with one of his friends who once studied at Akity University, who in turn introduced her to Akash, his fellow batchmate. Akash was working as a Project Fellow at LG Prasad Eye Institute, Hyderabad (Telangana), which is one of the world's best eye hospitals. Akash helped Prerna in getting appointments for her younger brother, Ramesh. Not only this, but he also generously offered support in lodging and assuring Ramesh get the best treatment possible. Prerna fell in love with his kindness and sense of humour. And Akash was moved by her commitment to help her brother get the best possible treatment for him. Their love story blossomed from that moment and Prerna often expressed her gratitude to Raghu for being the bridge that brought them together.

After spending just 24 hours with them, I quickly realised the importance of humour and being easy going with each other in a relationship. Akash has a fantastic sense of humour, which perfectly complements Prerna's fun-loving nature. Remarkably, Akash and Raghu hit it off despite having just met, and that connection made me appreciate Raghu even more. His ability to connect with others and his genuine willingness to help reflect his kind heart. It was heartwarming to see how laughter and light-heartedness could create such a positive atmosphere among us.

We started our day by visiting the Kasthamandap buddhist temple in Kathmandu, immersing ourselves in its serene atmosphere. It got damaged by an earthquake during 2015. Prerna recalled that many people came forward to donate blood in the temple premise to help the victims. Afterward, Prerna took us to her favourite breakfast spot, a quaint, old shop known for its *chana* (black chickpea) and dried *malpua* (a deep-fried dessert made with refined flour dough and sugar) served with tea. The meal was delicious, and the shop's nostalgic charm added to the experience. We took a few selfies amidst the backdrop of thousands of pigeons fluttering around us. We visited the ancient Hindu temples around, and we could see the damage caused by the 25 April 2015 earthquake. Raghuvendra's photography skills were impressive, capturing the essence of the moment perfectly.

With breakfast done, it was time for us to head to Pokhara. We first thought of taking a flight from Kathmandu, but later decided to enjoy the mountain ride, and also it helped lower our budget. We boarded a bus at around 1 PM, anticipating a four-hour journey. Little did we know, the trip would stretch into eleven hours due to unforeseen delays. The old bus rumbled and jolted along the dangerous mountain road, its weary tires struggling to find a combination on the uneven terrain just like us. This extended journey tested our patience and gave us a unique opportunity to see how we reacted to sudden changes in plans.

As the bus meandered through the scenic routes, we bonded over shared stories and laughter, making the most of our time together. The beautiful landscapes of Nepal unfolded outside our windows, providing a picturesque backdrop to our conversations. The bus creaked and groaned as it navigated the hairpin turns, while my thoughts mirrored the journey. Questions raced through my mind with each bump in the road bringing another wave of uncertainty.

❖ What if this date is a disaster?

❖ What if we discover we don't like each other as much as we think we do?

❖ What if, amid all this bumping and jolting, one of us stumbles and gets hurt, both physically and emotionally?

❖ What if our families somehow find out about this secret plan, and we have to face their judgement and disappointment?

❖ What if our lives come to a tragic end on this absurdly bumpy road?

These thoughts weigh heavily on my mind, making me as uncomfortable as the tires of the bus struggling over the muddy, uneven path. As the bus continued to shake and crawl, he reached out, maybe sensing my unease he gently took my hand. His touch held an unexpected comfort, and it temporarily eased my worries. We exchanged a knowing glance, a silent acknowledgment of the journey we were on, both on this bus and in our relationship. Our fingers laced together continued to offer silent companionship as the bus pressed forward. We found solace in conversation.

We did not realise when we switched gear from romance to spiritualism. He began to tell me about the new spiritual knowledge he had recently acquired from a friend in Bangalore. With enthusiasm he spoke with a sense of wonder, describing how it had reshaped his perspective on life and the world. His words were filled with a sense of awakening, and I couldn't help but listen intently. I realised there was so much more to him than I had ever imagined. He spoke of mindfulness and finding inner peace, which seemed so far removed from the chaotic road we were currently on.

As the sun began its slow descent, casting a golden hue over the rugged landscape, our bus continued its winding journey from Kathmandu to Pokhara. The initial excitement of the trip had gradually given way to a quiet calm. But, when the bus radio played the popular Nepali song "Oh Kajal," we all got back to our excited state. This song had quickly become our trip's anthem. Prerna, Akash, Raghuvendra, and I couldn't resist singing along, the lyrics on the tips of our tongues. At one point, we even created a fun reel.

Raghuvendra sitting next to me fixed his eyes on the breath-taking scenery outside. The terraced fields, quaint villages, flowing rivers and majestic mountains painted a picture of serene beauty. He occasionally pointed out interesting sights. Prerna and Akash were in the row beside us, engaged in a lively conversation. As dusk approached, the temperature dropped, and a cool breeze filtered through the slightly open windows.

As the day wore on, I began to feel a bit tired and found myself drifting off. Sensing my fatigue, Raghuvendra offered his lap as a pillow. We had naturally fallen into a rhythm of caring for each other, providing laps or shoulders whenever one of us needed a rest. Thanks to the unforeseen long tiring bus trip. With a playful smile, Raghuvendra suggested, "Imagine me to be your boyfriend for a day and feel free to rest on me." I laughed and accepted, settling my head on his lap.

We made a brief stop at a roadside tea stall. The driver announced a 20-minute break, and we all eagerly got off the bus to stretch our legs. After a few hours, there was another stop for our lunch past our lunch time but much before our dinner time. We ate *daal* (pulses, but often referred to soup made from pulses), *chawal* (rice), *sabji* (vegetables) and I guess some *pakoras* (veggies dipped in spiced chickpea flour and deep-fried), as well. I had heard that Nepali cuisine shares high resemblance with India, here I was witnessing it in Nepal. The bus again roared on the road, as the sky turned a deep shade of blue turning red, dotted with the first stars of the evening and a clear sight of the moon.

Back on the bus, the atmosphere grew more intimate as darkness fell. The only light came from the occasional passing vehicle. Suddenly, the bus wandered onto a path that could hardly be called a road. The way was rough, and we jolted with every bump. Out of nowhere, the conductor heard a disturbing noise and realised that the bus had lost all but one screw from the tire on Raghuvendra's side. The conductor quickly got to work, improvising by taking a screw from the remaining tires to fix the problem. Raghuvendra and Akash held their phones, using the torchlight to illuminate the scene for the conductor.

As I watched them work, my mind drifted to deeper thoughts about life's unpredictable journey. The bus's sudden breakdown mirrored the unexpected turns in our lives. I remembered how insecure I had felt about Raghuvendra initially, and now, here we were in Nepal, growing closer with each passing moment. What started as a regular conversation had blossomed into a meaningful connection, bringing us to this very place and moment.

As Raghuvendra and Akash re-joined us, Raghuvendra joked, "Imagine if the tire came off on my side, you'd all end up piled on top of me!" We all burst out laughing, the tension of the situation melting away. His ability to find humour in such a moment made me realise that he wasn't someone who got easily irritated by unexpected challenges. Instead, he faced them with a cheerful attitude. It also made me reflect on the times he had shared his struggles with me. Despite the challenges he had faced, Raghuvendra maintained his positive outlook, which spoke volumes about his strength and resilience. His way of handling adversity with a smile showed me the depth of his character and made me appreciate him even more. Conversations became softer, more personal. His genuine interest and thoughtful responses made me feel deeply connected to him.

The journey, though longer than expected, became a cherished memory. It was a blend of shared experiences and quiet moments, laughter and introspection. As the bus rolled on through the night, we were unaware of the adventures that awaited us in Pokhara.

That is how we spent day 2 of togetherness away from watchful eyes of our family and against the etiquette of conventional arranged marriage.

7. You're Courageous

Calling Raghuvendra and me a couple at that moment felt premature, yet we treaded towards that inevitable threshold.

It was midnight when we reached Pokhara after a bumpy bus ride and booked a cab to our hotel located near the lake area. The cab dropped us close to the hotel we had booked online. The rain was pouring hard, chilling me to the bone, soaking through my clothes. We were welcomed by clean roads and calm streets of Pokhara, yet there were street dogs to accompany us. Even though we had a hotel booked, we weren't happy with its appearance, so we decided to look for a better one. Prerna's concern mirrored Raghuvendra's insistence on comfort, especially given our rustic condition following a long bus ride. We carried all our bags and started searching for the right hotel. Raghuvendra and I each pulled a small trolley, while Prerna and Akash shared a larger one, showing the difference between married and unmarried couples. Calling Raghuvendra and me a couple at that moment felt premature, yet we treaded towards that inevitable threshold.

We started looking for hotels online and around. The place seems to have a lot of hotels. After having an uneasy pursuit through the rain-drenched streets, we gave up and decided to randomly sneak and seek information from whatever hotels we felt like inquiry worthy. We had walked almost 200 metres and decided to return back to the place where the cab had dropped us. We then went inside the hotel next to it and asked about availability. It looked very beautiful from outside yet not so luxurious. Our middle-class mind started thinking about escape plans if they ask for more or to think about ways to not look embarrassed even if we feel inside. Prerna went ahead and started interacting with the receptionist. The young guy with a very humbling conversation style was able to convince us to stay in the hotel. We took the elevator and went straight into our assigned rooms. Finally, we were in our hotel rooms after a reckless and hectic journey. It was a relief to be somewhere we can rest comfortably. After a hot shower, we climbed into bed and felt relaxed. We were on separate beds, watching some news on the television. When I turned towards Raghuvendra, he was already in deep sleep. I turned off the TV and reached out for my phone.

My phone had no signal all day, but as soon as I connected to hotel Wi-Fi, it flooded with WhatsApp notifications, including a missed call from mom. Since it was midnight, I decided to call her back in the morning. We were in a room with two king-size beds, and after such a tiring day, a hot shower made us quickly fall asleep. Morning had broken in Pokhara, bringing with it a crisp reminder of the pact Raghuvendra and I had made - to sleep in separate beds in hotels to avoid any awkwardness. And, here I was, on our first morning in this enchanting town, waking up beside Raghuvendra's bed who was still sleeping peacefully. I wanted to join him on his bed, touch his face and maybe hug or put my head on his chest and relax for a while before starting my day. But something stopped me, maybe the fear that we are still not sure about each other. And crossing boundaries would inflict pain. Stepping onto the balcony, the sight of cloud-dusted hills covered with ice greeted me, their dreamlike presence made my head blank and forget what, how and when going on in my life. The fresh, cold air invigorated me, and I returned to find Raghuvendra still nestled in bed. I set water to boil, preparing warm drinks for both of us to start our day. Thus began our journey in Pokhara, warmed by hot water and the chill of the morning air.

Excitement buzzed in the air as we prepared for our adventure in Pokhara, planned by our guide, Prerna. I dressed in a pink floral top paired with black jeans paired with a sling bag. I tied half of my hair back, leaving the rest to flow freely, paired with pink shoes and completed the look with light-brown lipstick. The cold air was a blessing for my dusky complexion, brightening my face and making me feel fresh and vibrant. Meanwhile, Raghuvendra chose a blue full-sleeve t-shirt, half shorts, and red shoes, adding a casual yet colourful touch to his outfit.

Prerna and Akash were already waiting for us downstairs, eager to embark on the day's adventure. As we hurried down to join them, the gentle patter of rain welcomed us, enveloping the surroundings in a misty, refreshing ambiance. The raindrops danced on the ground, and a cool breeze invigorated us, with a flicker of concern lingered—would the rain allow us to fully enjoy the day's plans?

With a hopeful assumption that the weather would soon clear, we ventured out into the rain, borrowing a large red umbrella from the hotel. It provided shelter from the drizzle as we made our way to a nearby cosy eatery for breakfast. The air was crisp and fresh, the rhythmic sound of raindrops on the umbrella creating a soothing melody above us.

At the corner where the street turned right into the market area, there was a small *Dhaba* (a roadside café or food stall) with wooden tables and chairs. A lady was preparing the food behind the chest height counter. It looked so homely. A middle-aged man with a very relaxed aura asked for what we prefer in our breakfast. They had *Aalo paratha* (potato pancake), *Paneer paratha* (cottage cheese pancake), *Pyaj paratha* (onion pancake) and egg rolls. Akash was excited about having *Aalo paratha*. We all tagged along with his choice and additionally, we ordered *Aalo paratha*. The first bite transported me back to India, the flavours remarkably familiar and comforting. The parathas were golden brown, crispy on the outside, and filled with a perfectly spiced potato mixture. All I could think of was green coriander *chutney* (a thick sauce of Indian origin that contains fruits, vinegar, sugar, and spices and is used as a condiment). or curd to complement it. However, we ended up with local *chutney* and pickles. Prerna and Raghuvendra also asked green chillies to add hotness with every bite of *paratha* into their mouth. The happy shop keeper kept bringing warm parathas and we kept them enjoying the early morning when rain poured through thin veils of sunlight. There was a drunk mid aged man sitting next to us, he kept asking for food, we offered a slice of paratha, he started eating. The shop owner saw it and immediately came to our table and suggested that we should not feed this drunk man. Whenever I see a poor or helpless person, I get emotionally frozen. I want to help them, but I don't know where to begin.

As usual, we paired our breakfast with tea—three cups without sugar and one with sugar, the latter unmistakably mine. The steam rose from the cups, blending with the rain-soaked air, creating a warm and inviting atmosphere. The tea was robust and fragrant, the perfect complement to our hearty breakfast. While the rain pattered around us, we savoured our meal, the taste and aroma bringing a sense of nostalgia and delight. It was a simple yet memorable start to our day, filled with the comforting flavours of home in a new and enchanting place. Our heart was happy and soul in the most relaxed state one can imagine. What can you ask more?

After the delicious breakfast we took a cab towards our first stop which was *Mahendra cave*, a large limestone cave discovered in 1950 by local shepherds, is a well-known attraction known for deep caves with a lot of bats. At the entrance, we paid for the ticket and received a handheld torch. Armed with the torch between the two of us, we led our group and began our short stroll down the stairs and descended steep steps into the main cave. The underground path was pitch dark, and our torch became indispensable. Thousands of bats hung quietly from the limestone ceiling, with just a few flying around. There was no natural light inside. The walls and ground were moist from the dripping water through the cracks and pores in the cave. Groups of people coming inside made noise breaking the natural silence of the cave. Prerna told us that the path out was not safe for small children or elderly people and the obese. Most of the group opted to return the way we came, but we were eager to experience the adventurous exit. Prerna led the way, squeezing through a small exit after climbing a slippery rock. It was a narrow hole with just enough space to squeeze out a person at once. One has to stand on one foot above a notch on the stone below and spread the arms outward pulling the whole trunk outside. Prerna had come here before, so we were comfortable following her. Prerna made her way out and now it was my turn. I was afraid but deep down there was a feeling of security with Prerna on the outside of the cave and Raghuvendra just behind me inside the cave. I struggled to find my footing on the slick surface; Raghuvendra offered his shoulder for support. Though worried I might be too heavy, I climbed onto his shoulders, making my way through the narrow exit. Raghuvendra and Akash followed suit, and together we emerged into the daylight, exhilarated by the experience. The adventure was challenging but immensely rewarding. I noticed my shoe prints on Raghuvendra's T-shirt, which made me feel both guilty and grateful. I brushed off the dust as best as I could with my bare hands. The moment we stepped out of the cave, we decided to capture a group photo.

Prerna and Akash excused themselves to use the restroom, leaving just the two of us outside. There was a large stone near the cave's entrance, on which Raghuvendra and I sat down, our backs resting against each other. It wasn't long before the discomfort set in, so I stood up to let him sit more comfortably.

But before I could fully rise, he grabbed my hand and tugged me back, nearly pulling me into his lap. I gasped, and in an instant, his arm wrapped around my shoulder, drawing me closer to him. My skin tingled with goosebumps, and I could feel my pulse quicken. He leaned in, his breath warm against my ear, and whispered, "You're courageous."

For a fleeting moment, I thought he might kiss me. I was sweating under the intensity of it all. In response, I slid my arm around his neck, a small gesture of affection, while his hand slipped down to my waist. The air between us thickened, and it felt like time had stopped.

Just then, we spotted Prerna and Akash walking back towards us. Embarrassed, we jumped up quickly, exchanging awkward smiles. Prerna, sensing the tension, tried to ease the moment. With a knowing smile, she suggested we take another photo, this time only two of us with the cave's exit as the backdrop. We gladly obliged, grateful for the distraction. Raghuvendra and I had an especially ecstatic picture together, where we looked as if we had known each other for a lifetime—a cherished memory that perfectly captures our bond. Many of my friends after looking at this pic expressed that we looked similar, our smiles and faces complemented each other. That picture remains one of our favourites; it's my WhatsApp DP and my laptop wallpaper, constantly reminding me of our beautiful connection.

By the time we emerged from the cave, it was already afternoon. We headed towards Phewa Lake, the iconic body of water in Pokhara. In both Nepali and Hindi, "Pokhara" (पोखरा) means "pond" or "lake." We decided to go boating on the lake, which stretches nearly 2.5 miles in length and 8.5 miles in width, with an average depth of 28 feet. The scenery was captivating—vibrant flowers, lush green hills, and a temple at the centre of the lake. The reflection of the mountains on the water's surface added to the breathtaking view, making it a popular spot for tourists and photographers alike.

The clouds were playing hide and seek, casting a sombre mood over the landscape. Boating, typically the best way to explore the lake's beauty, wasn't ideal today, as the looming clouds threatened to drench us at any moment. Each couple carried an umbrella, and for the first time, Raghuvendra and I shared one in the rain. It was a deeply romantic moment for us, something straight out of a movie or a love story—those moments we'd only imagined through the lens of cinema or heard about in legendary tales. Without the influence of movies, many of us might never have realised that walking or boating in the rain with your partner is considered romantic, haha. The sight of us huddled together, laughing and soaked, captured the pure joy of that moment. I felt no fear, uncertainty, or sense of being lost—only pure joy and bliss.

A funny incident happened during the boat ride. Prerna, trying to get us a lower fare, introduced us as Nepali. As soon as we sat in the boat, Raghuvendra, with a mischievous glint in his eye, started speaking in English with his distinct accent. The boater's eyes narrowed, and he began questioning our nationality, asking for identity proof. This comment made Akash's face flush with anger, and he snapped back, "Do you expect us to carry our passports around? You first show us your Nepali identity and a licence to operate this boat service". Raghuvendra emphasised that he is not a foreigner by speaking in Hindi. Prerna jumped amidst this conversation and started arguing that people from Terai region of Nepal speak Hindi and why should they carry passports. Prerna's husband is from Gorakhpur, an Indian district sharing a border with Nepal. Although she was reasonable with her argument, we knew we were trying to get away with paying foreign prices. Very soon, there was tension in the air which grew thicker. When we were all in the central docking landmass in the lake which accommodated the temple and a small garden; to our surprise, the boater pulled out a document, trying to intimidate us by saying that I can show my Nepali identity and licence to operate this boat.

Akash, not missing a beat, mockingly said, "Oh, it seems he does carry it."

We exchanged worried glances, almost ready to bribe him with extra money. But in the end, relief washed over us when we realised, he didn't have a passport himself, and we managed to laugh off the situation. When we got out of the boat, we realised that the guy returned us more money than justified. It seems he charged for just 3 heads. We recalculated and decided to return the extra money. We were very proud of our unequivocal ethical behaviour towards the boat driver, in spite of the fact that we had arguments with him. We also realised that we should not have lied about our nationalities. The mix of fear, guilt, honesty and amusement made the experience unforgettable.

After boating, we headed to a nearby restaurant in Pokhara for lunch. The restaurant was nestled in a narrow alley off the main road, but it opened up into a surprisingly spacious interior with a calming ambiance. It was an open dining arrangement with surroundings filled with a diversity of flowering and ornamental plants. The walls were adorned with handmade art, adding a touch of creativity and tranquillity to the setting.

A lady, who appeared to be in her mid-50s, approached us to take our order, followed closely by her husband, or so I believed. We ordered a *Thakali thali*, a traditional meal from the Thakali community in Nepal, that promised a delightful culinary experience. After taking our orders, the lady headed to the kitchen to prepare our food. Soon, the hot, sizzling *Thakali thali* was placed in front of us, filling the air with its mouthwatering aroma and promising a flavourful dining experience. We couldn't stop ourselves from praising its presentation. The vibrant colours and enticing aromas made our mouths water in anticipation. Prerna, with her phone, quickly snapped a picture of Raghuvendra and me, deliberately posing like hungry children holding our spoons, ready to dive into the feast with the hippo jumping in our stomach.

This *thali* was a balanced feast featuring a variety of dishes. One of the food items which surprised both me and Raghuvendra, was a very unfamiliar pickle, *palak ka aachar* (spinach pickle). The *bhindi (*okra fry) *bhujia* (pan-fried and steamed vegetable) spiced added a crispy, savoury element to the meal. Each component of the thali was carefully prepared to create a well-rounded, nutritious diet. The highlight was the *moong ka daal* (split moong soup), which was offered with a sizzling *ghee tadka* (tempering with clarified butter), infusing it with an irresistible aroma and rich flavour. The first serve was a warm, freshly made roti (Indian flat bread), which we eagerly tore into. This was followed by a generous bowl of steamed rice, providing a perfect base to savour the various curries and pickles.

After savouring the delicious food, we felt energised and ready for our next adventure. Prerna suggested we head towards the Sarangkot viewpoint to witness the Himalayan Mountain ranges by taking a cab. Since we were minutes away from the main road, we quickly got into a cab. The anticipation of the majestic mountains and the promise of stunning views spurred us on as we left the cosy restaurant behind. The path ahead beckoned with the allure of nature's grandeur, and we eagerly set out, ready to witness the beauty of the Himalayan range covered with snow. The cab dropped us off at a point where the road narrowed, and the driver guided us to walk for about 1 km, which led us to the stairs of a temple. As we climbed the last few stairs to enter into the temple premises, which was the gateway to the Sarangkot viewpoint, a local man asked for money as an entry fee. Prerna started arguing with him, insisting that demanding entry fee is illegal and that it was supposed to be free. The man quickly changed the topic, claiming it was a donation for temple maintenance. Prerna was really pissed off and started speaking in their local language, leaving us with no idea of what they were saying. Prerna refused to give him any money and moved forward, with us following her. The man kept babbling while Akash tried to calm Prerna down. We then entered the temple. Ahead of the temple was the Sarangkot viewpoint. We moved forward, and there it was—the Sarangkot viewpoint! It was so calm, with not a single hint of the hustle and bustle of busy life. But after a while when the clouds dispersed for a while, we could see the Pokhara airport and scattered tiny houses. The Himalayan range was completely covered by clouds, blocking the view, so we all decided to wait patiently until the clouds cleared. The most iconic among these Himalayan ranges is the *Machhapuchhre* mountain which sits in the Annapurna Mountain range of north-central Nepal. The name *Machhapuchhre* literally means "Fishtail" refers to the fish-tail-like shape of its twin summits. It has never been submitted due to some religious reasons.

Meanwhile, Raghuvendra decided to meditate for a while, mockingly saying "let me pray for the clouds to be removed.". Meanwhile, Akash and Prerna engaged in a lively conversation, their voices mingling with the natural sounds around us. Feeling a bit restless, I wandered off to explore the diverse array of wildflowers dotting the landscape. The vibrant colours and delicate petals provided a soothing distraction, each flower a tiny marvel in the overcast weather. The air was so fresh that it can't be explained in words. Despite our hopes, the sky did not clear, and we had to accept that we would not see the mountain ranges that day. After spending about two and a half hours, we began our journey back, feeling slightly disappointed but deeply enriched by the serene experience.

The other good thing was, Akash decided to give some money to the man with whom we'd argued earlier at the temple entrance. Akash believed that the man was genuinely trying to raise funds for the temple, even though his approach—pressuring people to donate by any means—was wrong. We didn't want to leave with any hard feelings, so we chose to end things on a positive note.

After returning we set off for a lakeside walk. The lake was serene, its waters calm and reflective. We walked beside it, not holding hands as there were still some invisible boundaries stopping us from showing a consistent lovely behaviour towards each other. While strolling by the lakeside, I spotted two huge cartoon characters, Mickey Mouse and Chhota Bheem, moving about and asking for money. The sight instantly transported me back to my childhood days when I was crazy about these characters. It was a delightful reminder of simpler times. I never thought that it could be a means of earning for someone. Funny thing is as kids, we can't even think of money being paid for acting or creating animations and movies. All we knew was money can bring chocolates, sweets, snacks, and new clothes.

Returning to the present moment, I soaked in the vibrant evening life of Pokhara. The lakeside was buzzing with travellers, each one eager to immerse themselves in the lively atmosphere. The lake side restaurants played music and displayed food items captivating the travellers. As we strolled along, we passed a restaurant offering chilled beer with a stunning view of the lake, but something else caught our attention—a small table where two ladies were selling "*bhutta*" (fresh maize roasted over a bonfire). The irresistible aroma drew us in, and we decided to indulge. The *bhutta*, with its tangy squeeze of lemon and a sprinkle of salt, was the perfect blend of flavours, both savoury and refreshing.

As we continued our walk, Prerna and Akash spotted a playful dog nearby. Its fur was soft, its tail wagging energetically, and its joy was contagious. The dog's antics lifted our spirits, and we couldn't resist capturing the moment with a photo. It was clear that Prerna and Akash were dog lovers. Seeing Prerna and Akash play with the dog brought back memories of my roommate, Simran. She was the one who taught me to love dogs and be kind to creatures that couldn't speak for themselves. Through her, I discovered the deep love these animals could give in return. Simran came into my life during a particularly low phase. She was an undergrad student while me being master's from the same university, I initially kept my distance, not sharing anything personal. We were both deeply immersed in our final year thesis work. She was an early sleeper, usually in bed by midnight, while I was a night owl, studying late into the night. My sleep schedule was erratic, with only four hours of rest as I would often study until 4 or 5 in the morning, rising at 7 for breakfast.

Despite our different schedules, we slowly became friends. Simran was overly dramatic and obsessed with daily soaps, particularly "*Bade Achhe Lagte Hain*," which she watched religiously. Yet, I couldn't help but admire her passion for the environment and her unwavering love for dogs. Her kindness and dedication to these causes made me see the world differently. Her genuine care for the environment and her boundless affection for animals showed me that love doesn't always have to be grand gestures; it can be found in the small, everyday acts of kindness. She brought a sense of warmth and compassion into my life, reminding me that even in the busiest of times, there is always room for love and care.

Now bringing you back to the lake side story. Later in the evening, we witnessed an *aarti* (a Hindu ritual employed in worship) ceremony by the lake, reminding me of the Ganga *aarti* at *Varanasi*. The scene was vibrant, with ladies and men dancing in spiritual devotion around the aarti and their colourful attire. The flickering oil lamps cast a warm, golden light, illuminating its warmth in the surrounding. Raghuvendra went ahead to capture the moment with his camera, while Prerna, Akash, and I enjoyed the spectacle from a distance. The air was filled with a sense of spirituality and magic, the rhythmic chants blending with the sounds of the lake. When it came time to take the aarti, we approached the spiritual fire, feeling the magical warmth amidst the cold weather. All four of us took the aarti, but Raghuvendra, with his phone in hand, used only one hand. It felt incomplete to me, so I took his phone and insisted he take the *aarti* properly with both hands. He smiled, appreciating the gesture. The evening ended on a note of laughter and spiritual fulfilment. The warmth of the *aarti* lingered in our hearts as we embraced the magical experience by the lakeside. The lake shimmered in the moonlight, and the silhouette of the mountains stood majestically in the background, completing the picturesque scene.

After the *aarti*, a light drizzle began, cooling the evening air. We hurried toward the nearest shelter, which turned out to be a small shop. Only when we stepped inside did we realise it was an alcohol shop. The faint smell of spirits lingered in the air, and out of curiosity, we found ourselves browsing the various bottles lined up on the shelves.

Raghuvendra's eyes lit up as he scanned the beer section. I knew he loved beer, though I wasn't much of a drinker myself. The one time I had tried alcohol, it had been just a spoonful of brandy—enough to taste but not enough to savour. Akash and Raghu's attention was now glued to a particular shelf packed with different types of beer, their interest piqued. I watched them with a quiet smile, amused by how quickly they had gravitated toward their shared fascination. They decided to try "GORKHA" beer, a renowned Nepali brand recommended by one of Raghuvendra's Nepali friends.

Seeking a pleasant spot to enjoy our drinks, we chose a restaurant with a fantastic roadside view and settled on the balcony, which offered an amazing vantage point. We were not sure if the restaurant would allow drinks from outside, but the girl attending us was so nice to allow us. From our dining table, we could witness the roadside adorned with colourful banners and twinkling lights, creating a lively atmosphere as travellers strolled by, enjoying the evening. Raghuvendra and Akash went to get more beer while Prerna and I chatted, getting to know each other better. She turned out to be a kind and caring person, sharing amusing stories about her and Raghuvendra's time during their masters' days in Japan. There were times when Prerna praised Raghuvendra for his kindness and helpful nature, which made me feel good learning more about him.

Raghuvendra and Akash soon returned, and they looked very excited like kids. Very soon we found ourselves ordering some *chakhna* (some snacks which are often served to complement alcoholic beverages) — crispy *papad* (a thin roasted pancake usually made from any kind of legumes flour. In the main course, we ordered an assortment of delicious *momos* (Indian/Nepali dumplings). The *momos* turned out to be incredibly captivating. It's said that *momos* originated in Tibet and were brought to Nepal by Tibetan immigrants who settled in the Kathmandu Valley. In India, *momos* gained popularity through the Nepali community, and I was fascinated to learn that under the 1950 Indo-Nepal Treaty of Peace and Friendship, Nepalese citizens can live and work freely in India.

As I took my first bite, my mouth was filled with a burst of spices, and I couldn't help but relish the experience. These were authentic, true to their roots, with a rich aroma. The *momos* were even better when paired with the restaurant's sauces, which added a perfect blend of tangy and spicy notes. As night fell, a sudden power cut turned the restaurant into darkness. The staff there quickly provided us candles, transforming our casual dinner into a romantic candlelit one. The soft glow of the candles illuminated Raghuvendra's face, making him look even more stunning, with a touch of intoxicated charm.

The soft sound of raindrops and the cool breeze created a peaceful setting. The warmth of the hot *momos* was a perfect contrast to the chilly air, making each bite feel comforting. The flickering candlelight added a cosy, golden glow to our table. The mix of the scenic rain, the cool breeze, and the steaming, fragrant *momos* made the evening truly memorable. It was so romantic, but the food was equally tempting.

After our delightful dinner, we wandered around, indulging in some late-night shopping. Being minimalists, Raghuvendra wanted to buy just a few postcards to share with his friends, and he later gave me half of them (was I his closest one? Haha). On our way back, we stumbled upon a man selling *paan* (betel nut) from his bicycle. Chewing betel nut leaves mixed with spices and sweets, known as *paan*, is a cultural tradition in both Nepal and parts of India. Akash and Raghuvendra eagerly bought one for themselves, while I inquired about the fiery fire *paan*.

Fire *paan* is made by placing a combustible substance over *paan* and then lighting it up. The seller quickly pops the burning *paan* into the mouth of the consumer. When I decided to try it, Prerna was shocked and exclaimed, "*Are, jal jayega*! (Oh no, your mouth might burn!)" But I went ahead, relishing the thrill of the unique experience.

We continued to wander through the lively streets, absorbing the vibrant energy of the night, before finally returning to our hotel. We took a shower in turn and slipped inside our blankets. This time on the same bed but still there was a physical boundary between us. Exhausted from a long day, we fell asleep immediately. Thus ended our first day in Pokhara—a day full of unexpected joys and unforgettable moments.

8. The Budding Romance

The rain intensified, but we embraced it, singing and dancing in the downpour.

In the quiet of the morning, my alarm abruptly stirred me from sleep—a reminder of my resolve to rise early, unlike the day before. I moved with purpose, preparing myself swiftly for the day ahead. The night had stretched long, filled with conversation with Supriya, the one friend back in India who knew about this trip. Supriya was about three years younger than me, and she was someone who was always positive about my future with Raghuvendra even when our relationship was going through tough times and uncertainty. Since this journey was a secret, I had chosen to keep it to myself, sharing it only with her.

Supriya's concern surfaced in a simple question: Did I harbour any regrets or emotional turmoil during my time in Nepal? Until that moment, I hadn't paused to consider it, but her words stirred something deep within me. Suddenly, I found myself tangled in thought, wrestling with emotions I hadn't fully acknowledged and a growing sense of confusion. I glanced at my phone—it was around 2 AM. While Raghuvendra slept peacefully beside me, I couldn't quiet my mind. Hoping to find some relief, I went to the bathroom, splashing cool water on my face. The chill offered a momentary calm, but as I returned to bed, my thoughts persisted. The late hour only deepened my restlessness, and it was much later when I finally drifted off, still grappling with the emotional undercurrents that Supriya's questions had brought to the surface.

I began the morning with a warm glass of water, offering the same to Raghuvendra as the soft glow of early sunlight filtered through the curtains. After freshening up, I put on my outfit: a black spaghetti top paired with a blue printed open shirt and grey Jeggings. I completed the look with a delicate pendant and matching earrings, gifted by

Raghuvendra back in Delhi. As I admired my reflection, Raghuvendra remarked that I looked like a young college girl, bringing a smile to my face.

Raghuvendra dressed in a crisp full shirt and pants, ready for the day's adventures. With time to spare, I started taking mirror selfies, capturing the morning's quiet charm. Raghuvendra soon joined in, and we took a few cute selfies together. Embracing his role as my personal photographer, Raghuvendra encouraged me to pose. He captured me holding the curtain with a soft, shy smile as the sunlight framed my face. This photo, taken by Raghuvendra, became and still remains my Fakebook display picture—a cherished memory of a perfect morning. In those moments, I even forgot the turmoil that had consumed me the night before, spurred by conversations with Supriya. It's interesting how the night can amplify our worries, turning simple situations into complex dilemmas. Yet, it also offers a solitary space for reflection, though often we end up overthinking, losing sight of the clarity that dawn can bring.

After our photoshoot, we checked on Prerna and Akash, who were nearly ready. We left the hotel together, stepping into the fresh morning air, and decided to stop for breakfast. This time, we wanted to try a different eatery. We found another roadside shop and chose a table with a view of the street, which had not yet reached its crowd peak. We ordered the same holy *Aalo paratha* with *masala* (spice) tea. The parathas were tasty, but there was nothing offered to complement them—no *chutney,* pickles, or anything to dip them in. We were a bit disappointed in the moment, but the anticipation of our upcoming trek kept us going.

After finishing breakfast, we hopped onto a public bus that took us on a brief ride to Devi's Fall. When we arrived, the powerful rush of water greeted us with its thunderous roar. From a distance, the waterfall appeared to be a calm stream, but as we drew nearer, we discovered it plunging into a vast cave. Unlike most waterfalls that cascade from a height, Devi's Fall is unique—an underground waterfall.

The intensity of the water created a dramatic atmosphere, with the force so immense that it made the ground around it vibrate. Raghuvendra was visibly awestruck by the sheer beauty and power of this extraordinary phenomenon. For both of us, this was our first encounter with an underground waterfall. Local lore suggests that the water vanishes into an eternal underground world after flowing through a nearby *Gupteshwor Mahadev Cave*, often referred to as the "cave beneath the ground.". It felt as if a colossal cavern was swallowing an immense volume of water, adding to the waterfall's mystique and grandeur.

Devi's Fall is steeped in history and legend. On July 31, 1961, a Swiss woman named Mrs. Davi (or Davis) tragically drowned here after being swept away by the strong currents while swimming in Phewa Lake. Her body was recovered three days later from the Phusre River, which is connected to the waterfall. The site was later named "Devi's Fall" in her memory. Locally, the waterfall is also known as *"Patale Chango,"* which translates to "Underworld's Waterfall," a name that reflects the mysterious and powerful nature of this underground cascade. Devi's Fall, with its compelling history and dramatic beauty, is one of the most visited attractions in Nepal. A few hundred metres from the waterfall, we visited a statue garden where we took photos among statues of Nepali couples in traditional attire. The statues had face holes designed for visitors to insert their faces, creating a playful way to blend into the scenes while hiding our bodies. We posed for a few pictures, though amidst the fun, we were still uncertain about our future together and whether we would actually become husband and wife.

After marvelling at the enchanting Devi's Fall, we made our way to the nearby *Gupteshwor Mahadev Cave*. The entrance of the cave exuded a mysterious allure, making it feel like we had stepped into another world. The water from Devi's Fall flowed through the cave, and the cave itself was a labyrinth of intricate, naturally formed rock formations shaped over time. Although the cave had been equipped with some artificial lighting and paved pathways for visitor convenience, it retained its ancient charm.

As we ventured deeper, the dim lighting and cool, damp air created a sense of adventure. The complex rock formations and the echo of our footsteps amplified the cave's mystical atmosphere. Emerging from the cave, we felt a profound connection to Nepal's ancient and mystical heritage, our experience deeply enriched by the natural beauty and historical significance of the site.

It was time for our hill adventure. We boarded a local bus and headed towards the trail entrance for a hike to the World Peace Pagoda and Pumdikot Shiva Statue. Known as one of the best short and easy hikes in Pokhara, it promised a blend of scenic beauty and tranquillity. This hike offers a stunning view of Phewa Lake, the Annapurna, Dhaulagiri, Machhapuchchhre, Hiunchuli, and Manaslu Mountain ranges, encompassing green hills, curvy roads, and beautiful mountainous villages. We were uncertain which bus to take, but after a few confusing moments, Prerna finally figured it out. The bus dropped us about 2 kilometres away from the trail entrance. We took this opportunity to walk and visit a cave temple dedicated to Hindu gods, an underground temple with many stairs. We explored it for nearly an hour. Around the temple, there were numerous shops selling souvenirs, traditional clothes, and local food.

We then continued toward the trail entrance. On the way, we saw shops selling *samosas* (triangular pastry with a savoury filling, mostly vegetables, spiced potatoes, onions. The entire pastry is deep-fried in vegetable oil to a golden brown) and *jalebis* (deep-fried intersecting ring-shaped desserts made using fermented refined flour which are then soaked in sugar syrup). Initially, we resisted, but eventually, Raghuvendra and Akash couldn't pass up the sugary jalebis. They wanted fresh and crisp ones, and finally, they spotted a sweet shop across the road. Prerna gave some Nepali currency to Raghuvendra for the purchase, but he realised he was 40 Nepali rupees short. He managed by paying with Indian rupees instead. For decades, India and Nepal have maintained a constant currency conversion rate of 1 INR equivalent to 1.6 Nepali rupees, showing a deeper historical relationship between the two nations. While Indian currency is commonly accepted along the border areas, it is not always accepted in interior areas. Luckily, the sweet shop vendor accepted Indian rupees. We decided to eat them during our first break of the hike.

We began our hike, passing through small villages and houses with very few people. Many youths in the region often migrate to bigger cities or abroad in search of better livelihoods. The stairs were steep, slowing our pace at the beginning. Twenty minutes into our walk, we stopped to devour our *jalebis* under a resting spot beneath a giant tree. From there, we could see the beautiful city of Pokhara and the winding roads disappearing into the mountains. Raghuvendra opened the bag of *jalebis* and excitedly invited everyone to join in. They were cold yet crunchy and not overly sweetened. As we chatted about nature, trees, mountains, and *jalebis*, we suddenly noticed a playful puppy barking at us from a nearby house.

We also saw chestnut trees, which neither Raghuvendra nor I had seen before. Raghuvendra asked Prerna if they were edible, and upon her confirmation, he plucked some fruits from the thorny plant. He cracked open the fruit with a stone, and we enjoyed freshly plucked chestnuts for the first time. Raghuvendra was thrilled to have discovered this new fruit tree. He shared that when he was in Japan, he once bought roasted chestnuts from local farmers on his way to a hike, making this a nostalgic and relishing moment for him.

It was time to trek ahead. We had just moved 100 metres when we saw a square resting structure made of stone and bricks. It looked like an old, no-longer-used resting place for hikers. While I was looking at it, Prerna noticed and started explaining that this used to be a resting spot for people carrying goods to the mountaintop. There were many such operational resting spots across the trails. Being from the plains of Bihar, I could only appreciate the mental and physical toughness of the people from the mountains.

Chatting, singing, and laughing, we arrived at the World Peace Pagoda, also known as the Pokhara Shanti Stupa, perched on Anadu Hill. The concept of the World Peace Pagoda originated from the vision of Buddhist monk Nichidatsu Fujii, who sought to promote peace and unity. Fujii, founder of the Buddhist organisation Nipponzan Myohoji, believed that constructing such stupas worldwide could contribute to global peace.

In 1947, he began building peace houses as sanctuaries for world peace, with the first World Peace Pagodas emerging in Nagasaki and Hiroshima in Japan as symbols of hope and tranquillity following the devastation of the nuclear bombings. Today, about 80 Peace Pagodas exist across Asia, Europe, and the Americas, with the Pokhara Peace Pagoda being the 71st of these stupas.

We joined the many visitors who wandered around and entered the pagoda to pray. After spending some time in reflection and relaxation within the pagoda's serene premises, we decided to move to the opposite side, where the shade offered a pleasant resting spot away from harsh sunlight. The weather was very hot making our stay uncomfortable. So we decided to move and decide where to go next. While getting down the stairs from the pagoda, Raghuvendra and I decided to get some pictures taken. He put his hand on my shoulder, and feeling shy, happy, and a bit nervous, I held him close by wrapping my left arm around his waist. I think we already looked amazing together.

From the right side of the Pagoda towards Phewa Lake, a small trail branches off, leading up to the Shiva statue at the top of the mountain. Prerna, feeling a bit tired, asked if we still wanted to continue, mentioning that she had never gone beyond this point before. Without hesitation, we all decided to push onward.

We began our walk, taking in the sights of the green valley, winding roads, chickens roaming freely, and the sky, mountains, and houses along the way. The path ahead turned from a proper road into a muddy trail winding through the terrain. We jumped onto the trail, our excitement growing with each step. The journey was tiring but thrilling, and we hardly encountered any other travellers along the way. Though there was a road that also led tourists to the Shiva statue, we chose the less-travelled path, which made the experience even more fun. Every now and then, we paused to catch our breath and admire the stunning views.

Finally, we reached our destination. We were greeted by a large statue of Shiva, but what truly caught my attention was the depiction of Ganesha, Shiva's son, circling the statue on his vehicle, a mouse. This scene reminded of a story from Hindu mythology where Shiva challenges his sons, Kartikeya and Ganesha, to complete three rounds of the world, promising to declare the winner as the wisest one. Kartikeya, riding his peacock, swiftly flies off to circle the world. Meanwhile, Ganesha simply completes three rounds around their parents, declaring that they are his entire world. Ganesha's victory was not achieved through physical feats but through the depth of his understanding and devotion, as he recognized his parents as his world. This revelation illustrates that true triumph lies in spiritual insight and familial love.

The sight of Shiva standing tall and majestic against the backdrop of the mountains filled us with a deep sense of spirituality and reverence for the god of destruction and the first Yogi. Being among the few who hiked to this spot, we celebrated our achievement, knowing it wasn't a common feat for most people. The air was filled with joy and laughter as we soaked in the serene presence of the statue. We watched people worshipping Shiva, kids playing nearby, and felt a profound connection to the spiritual and natural beauty of Nepal. We went inside, prayed with folded hands for a while, and roamed around to witness the magnificent landscape of Pokhara from the hilltop.

It was almost 3 pm and the sky was getting cloudy, so Prerna suggested trekking back as rain would create trouble. We retraced our steps along the trail and arrived at the intersection where the trail met the paved road that leads travellers to the Shiva statue. There was a small eatery there, with a lady inside waiting for customers. She was selling noodles, *momos*, milk tea, snacks, biscuits, and *pakoras*. We enjoyed some tea and *momos*, taking a moment to relax and unwind. Very soon, the sky started to drizzle so we squeezed under the tin roof of the small eatery to avoid getting wet. But it was getting darker so we had to move fast to reach down to the plains. Given the worsening weather, we considered taking a bus or renting a car, but our attempts were unsuccessful, so we continued trekking down the hill. The rain intensified, but we embraced it, singing and dancing in the downpour. Raghuvendra, using his waterproof phone, captured our fun moments on video, including a few dancing clips.

By the time we reached the Stupa area, the rain and clouds had completely obscured our view. We could barely see beyond 20 metres. We decided to take shelter in a tea shop that, on sunny days, might have offered a great view of the landscape. We looked at the menu and smiled when we saw that a cup of milk tea was priced at 250 Nepali rupees—much more than we expected. Opting for a more affordable black tea at 150 Nepali rupees, we got a simple tea bag dipped in warm water. The preparation was basic, but we didn't complain. Being able to enjoy a warm cup of tea while sitting on top of a mountain in the rain felt like a blessing.

After an hour, the rain became calm. We were all drenched and wanted to rush back to our hotel to change our clothes and feel warm. We quickly made our way out of the trails and called a cab. We arrived back at our hotel and changed our clothes. It was an amazing day. Both Raghuvendra and Prerna were amazed by my resilience during the hike. I did not feel tired or exhausted, probably because the company of people who make you feel happy makes a difference in our lives, not just during a hike. I was proud of myself and happy that I could keep pace with Raghuvendra, who is a crazy hike lover.

Returning from the hike, we were all soaked from the rain, having been drenched twice by the persistent downpour. After taking a shower, changing into dry clothes, and fully drying ourselves, Raghuvendra was standing next to me, looking for something interesting on TV. I was slouched with my neck down and my back arched like a hump. Raghuvendra noticed this and began correcting my posture—something I hadn't considered problematic before. He suggested I should walk straighter and not lean my neck forward. He approached close to me, holding me by my shoulder and neck, correcting my posture. It was sure, we had become comfortable touching each other. His touch became more tender, and his gestures more affectionate. The way he gently adjusted my posture, his hands lingering a bit longer, made it clear that he was becoming more romantic. The warmth of his touch contrasted with the sound of rain on the outside, creating a moment that felt both intimate and nurturing.

Being shy, I followed his advice like a child listening to a guardian, trying to emulate his example. I realised this habit of mine had likely developed from spending countless hours hunched over books in the library, my head bowed in concentration. He really cared for people around him, it was reflected on many occasions. I don't remember if anyone noticed or even bothered to point to my wrong posture. It's surprising how we can develop habits unconsciously and only recognize them when someone points them out. Unfortunately, many people today shy away from pointing out bad habits in those close to them, not because they are unkind, but because most people prefer to avoid confrontation. When someone highlights our bad habits, we often react in different ways:

- ❖ Some are eager to improve, viewing it as an opportunity for self-betterment.

- ❖ Others dismiss it, considering it a minor issue that doesn't need much effort.

- ❖ Some perceive it as criticism rather than constructive feedback.

Improvement is certainly challenging, but it's essential to approach it with a positive mindset. From my own experience, I was blind to many of my bad habits—often choosing to remain blind. Not knowing about issues in oneself is one thing, but knowing our flaws and ignoring or avoiding working on them is self-toxic.

Feeling warm after a while, we decided to step out of our hotel for dinner. We returned to the cosy restaurant where we had shared *momos* and GORKHA beer before and ordered a vegetarian *thali* (platter). Sitting at the same table with the charming balcony view, we enjoyed our meal together. The familiar ambiance and delicious food made everything feel perfect. This time, Raghuvendra and I were more comfortable with each other, and we didn't miss any chance to show our affection.

As we walked back to our hotel, I could feel the invisible walls between us melting away. He rested his hands on my shoulders, and I gently wrapped my arm around his waist, bringing us closer. My face nestled against his chest, and we walked in sync, completely connected, leaving no space between us. We were finally letting go of our old boundaries, ready to become one.

As we reflected on the day, we realised how fulfilling and adventurous it had been. The thrill of the hike, the laughter we shared, and the quiet moments of connection all wove together into a beautiful tapestry of memories. Our second day in Pokhara ended on a satisfying note, and it was also going to be our last night in the city. We returned to our hotel, exhausted. We jumped onto the same bed, and I rested my head on his arms and gradually on his chest. Before we knew it, it was already morning.

9. Revelation

In the morning, as the train reached Varanasi, I felt a wave of relief wash over me—our secret trip had finally come to an end.

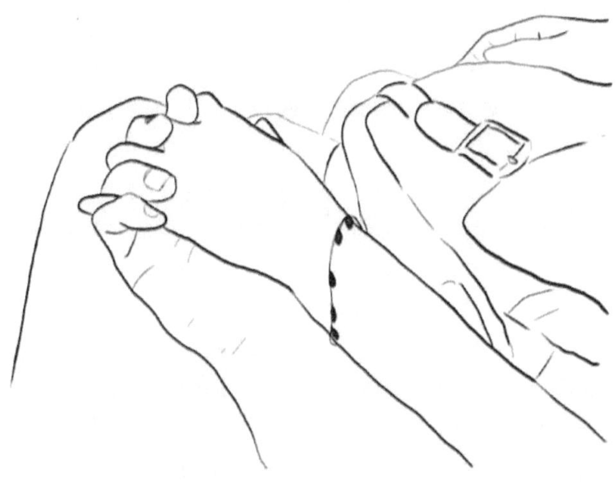

Finally, our trip to Pokhara was coming to an end. Though the journey hadn't gone exactly as planned— many activities were interrupted by rain—Prerna assured us that we had covered most of the key spots wisely.

Despite the weather, it had been a fulfilling adventure. The day before, Prerna had informed us that we would be returning to Kathmandu by the same bus. Preparing ourselves for the bumpy ride, we donned our most comfortable clothes for those 12 hours long journey. My skin had tanned from the trekking, leaving me looking a bit dull. On the other hand, Raghuvendra, exhausted from the busy schedule, was feeling feverish.

I chose a simple short kurti paired with jeans and belly shoes, while Raghuvendra opted for a t-shirt and shorts. Our casual attire matched our mood for the long journey back. After packing up and vacating our room, we double-checked everything before heading downstairs. To our surprise, we discovered that we wouldn't be taking the bus after all. Instead, we would be flying back to Kathmandu—a quick 25-minute flight. This unexpected change lifted our spirits, promising a more comfortable journey and an opportunity to have an aerial view of the snow-covered mighty Himalayan ranges. At the Pokhara airport, we faced another delay—our flight was postponed by two hours. The weather was cloudy, preventing airlines from landing safely. Nepal has a poor history of aeroplane crashes due to difficult geography, and poor safety measures, among many reasons. In January 2023, 72 people were killed when a plane crashed on approach to the city of Pokhara. But, for some reason we were not worried about anything, and felt perfectly safe. We settled into the waiting area, using the time to review the numerous photos we had taken during our trip. The memories flashed before us, each picture telling a story of laughter, exploration, and bonding.

To pass the time, we played a few rounds of the Ludo game on our phone, our competitive spirits turning the waiting period into a fun-filled interval. Engrossed in the game, we didn't even notice the hours slipping by. After a while, we went through the security check and moved towards the gate. The anticipation buzzed among us as we sat, eagerly awaiting our flight. From where we sat, the view was great: mountain ranges framed the horizon, their peaks kissed by the morning sun playing hide and seek due to moving clouds. The sight from Pokhara airport was a perfect farewell to the picturesque town.

As we boarded the plane, we initially found our seats placed apart. However, with a bit of luck, we managed to sit together. I took the window seat with Raghuvendra beside me, while Prerna and Akash were in parallel seats across the aisle. We chatted lightly, the fatigue of the past days evident in our voices. By now, Raghuvendra and I had grown so comfortable with each other that sitting hand in hand felt natural, with no trace of awkwardness. At one point, Prerna teased us, saying she could "feel the love in the air," which left both of us blushing. I couldn't bring myself to look at him, instead finding myself shyly smiling at the ground.

Raghuvendra, not feeling well, soon grew sleepy and rested his head back. I gazed out of the window, lost in thought. Suddenly, the clouds parted, and there they were—the Himalayan ranges, floating majestically above the clouds. The peaks seemed almost within reach, their snow-capped summits gleaming in the sunlight. It was as if nature was rewarding us for our journey. Raghuvendra, despite his weariness, managed to capture a few stunning images of the mountains, each click preserving the magic of that moment.

The flight was remarkably short, feeling like a blink compared to the eight-hour bus ride we had initially anticipated. The contrast between the two journeys was stark—one filled with the slow, rhythmic bumps of the road, the other a swift, smooth glide through the sky. Each journey held its own set of memories, adding to the richness of our trip. We landed in Kathmandu around 10 am, the familiar hustle and bustle welcoming us back. As we stepped out of the airport, a sense of completion washed over us. The trip to Pokhara had been a perfect mix of planned activities and spontaneous adventures, rain-soaked hikes, and serene moments. Each experience, whether smooth or challenging, had brought us closer and enriched our journey in ways we hadn't anticipated.

After reaching Kathmandu, we booked a cab and headed straight to Boudhanath. The drive was filled with quiet anticipation, concern and fatigue. Raghuvendra's fever started taking over him, while Prerna suffered from a cold and the rest of us were also feeling tired. Thankfully, I had brought some medicines with me, which Raghuvendra took. I always carry a few essential medicines and balm when travelling; you never know who might need what. As we reached Boudhanath, Prerna, gaining wisdom, took 2 international tickets for me and Raghuvendra and two Nepali tickets for her and her husband. As we steeped in the history and legend of Boudhanath, it captivated us from the moment we arrived. There are a large number of Buddhist settlements around the temple area.

Following the 1959 Tibetan uprising, a large number of the Tibetan refugees migrated to Nepal and settled down around Boudhanath. The site, originally called "*Khasti Mahachaitya*", which means "great stupa of the dew drops". Later, the government renamed it Boudhanath to better reflect Nepal's Hindu heritage, where "Natha" is used in different religious contexts. There is an interesting story behind this temple. According to legend, the stupa was built by a prince to honour his father, King Akashaditya, after his sacrifice to bring water to the kingdom. This Buddhist holy site is said to house the relics of Kassapa Buddha, one of the five Buddha from present *Kalpa* (a very long period of time in Hindu and Buddhist cosmology, usually in billions of years) who came before Gautam Buddha. A *Kalpa* is a very long period of time in Hindu and Buddhist cosmology, usually in billions of years, generally between the creation and recreation of a universe.

As we approached the stupa, we were greeted by a sea of colourful prayer flags fluttering in the breeze. Despite our fatigue, we couldn't help but be captivated by the sheer beauty and spiritual energy of the place. The stupa stood tall, its white dome and golden spire gleaming under the sunlight. Walking around the stupa, we took in the vibrant atmosphere. Pilgrims and tourists alike circled the structure, spinning prayer wheels and murmuring chants. The air was thick with the scent of incense and the soft hum of prayers, creating a sense of peace and reverence. We wandered through the surrounding area, exploring small shops filled with intricate handicrafts, colourful *thangkas* (a form of Buddhist art that are used in temples and monasteries to support Buddhist practices), and traditional Tibetan jewellery. The energy of Boudhanath was so serene. We embraced the beauty and history of this sacred site, feeling a deep connection to the countless pilgrims who had come before us.

The sun was already high overhead, and it was very hot. We started feeling hungry while carrying our bags. We took a few photographs, admiring the beauty of the Stupa. One of the most memorable pictures of Raghuvendra and me together is the one where I'm hiding my face behind Raghuvendra's shoulder, holding his face, and he's wrapping his arms around my shoulders. We looked so close in that picture. Our eye caught a glimpse at the board on a building right in the front of the stupa displaying "Tibetan food". We quickly went inside, climbed the stairs to eat a lot of food. As usual, a balcony seat with a clear view of the stupa was chosen by us. Despite the pleasant ambiance, the service was poor, though the food tasted nice. We tried different types of *momos* and some famous Tibetan dishes. Some of the dumplings had very similar taste compared to ones we had in Pokhara. One of the unique dishes was "*Laphing*," a spicy cold noodle dish garnished with chilli oil, soy sauce, and vinegar. Another was "*thukpa*", a combination of

Tibetan-style noodles with vegetables stew in clear soup. Each dish was delicious, and we also enjoyed the famous Nepali *momos*. Everything was new to me, except for the steamed and fried dumplings, but even with them the stuffings were different to what I used to have back in India. The sauce with dumplings was not spicy in Nepal, this is in contrast to what I used to have back in India, the very spicy red sauce served with dumplings. The serving size was so large that it was difficult for us to finish, but we savoured every bite, feeling wonderfully full. By the end of the meal, Raghuvendra's fever had subsided, and he looked much better. It was time to head to the airport for our flight back to Delhi.

As we drove towards the airport, through the bustling streets of Kathmandu, Prerna shared some poignant stories about Nepal. She talked about how many Nepalis go abroad to earn a living or pursue education, leaving behind heartbroken families. The sight of newlyweds parting ways or young children crying for their fathers was a common, yet deeply emotional scene. At the airport, we saw a teenage boy, likely heading abroad for his studies, being given a green garland, a cultural symbol of farewell and good luck. Prerna and Akash had decided to stay in Kathmandu for a while longer with her family, she called her younger brother, Ramesh to pick her from the airport, and bring some fresh *"Jalebis"* for us. Ramesh arrived quickly with a lot of *"Jalebis"*. We ate till our hearts, talking about many things we can't really recall.

We were so engrossed in our conversation that time flew by, and soon it was time for our final goodbye to Prerna and Akash. We took a few group photographs, capturing the end of our memorable trip. Prerna remarked how much fun she had with me, and I felt a wave of gratitude for the entire experience. The trip, with all its ups and downs, had brought us closer and left us with unforgettable memories. Leaving them behind, we stepped into the Kathmandu airport, a mix of emotions swirling within us. The airport was a hive of activity, with travellers' faces reflecting anticipation, fatigue, and excitement. We found a quiet corner and settled in to wait for our flight. The departure announcement broke our reverie, and soon we were boarding the plane for the two-hour journey back to New Delhi.

The flight itself felt like a transition between two worlds. The memories of cool mountain air and serene landscapes contrasted sharply with the anticipation of Delhi's heat. As we descended, the city lights of Delhi spread out below us like a glittering concrete forest. The temperature hit us as soon as we stepped off the plane, a wave of heat that was a stark reminder of our return to reality which comes with "great human development". As I stepped off the plane, my phone buzzed to life, finally reconnecting to the network after five days of silence. Notifications poured in, a flood of messages and missed calls, pulling me back into the rhythms of everyday life.

Navigating through the airport, we made our way to the metro. The ride was filled with a comfortable silence, Raghuvendra and I chatted a bit and then each of us lost in our thoughts, reflecting on the trip's highs and lows. The metro journey, with its rhythmic clatter and occasional announcements, was soothing in its familiarity. We arrived at my place late at night. On our way back we ordered *biryani* (a South Asian dish combining Indian spicy rice and *Persian polao (Pulaf)*, made with basmati rice, meat, fish, eggs, or vegetables, and infused with aromatic spices) for dinner. We gathered around the table, eating biryani while talking with each other about some random stuff about the trip. As we ate, the exhaustion of the journey began to catch up with us. The conversation was light, interspersed with laughter and shared recollections of our trip. After dinner, the weariness became too much to ignore. Drifting off to sleep, I felt a deep gratitude for the experiences we had shared. The journey had been more than just a vacation; it had been a collection of moments that had brought us closer, enriched our lives, and left us with stories to tell. And with that comforting thought, I slipped into a deep, restful sleep, the warmth of the Delhi night wrapping around me like a blanket; and forcing me to turn on the air conditioner.

In the morning, I woke up around 7, recovering from the exhaustion of previous days. Raghuvendra was already awake by then and had finished brooming the marbled floor and began gathering his dirty clothes from the trip to wash. I handed him mine as well. He loaded the washing machine and then went for a bath. In rural India, it's common for men to work outside while household chores are traditionally managed by women, whereas normally men don't help in household chores. Although this is gradually changing, these roles remain deeply rooted in our culture. Watching Raghu assist with household tasks at my place made me admire him even more, as I never saw a very clear division of labour back in my home. My aunt, who is a high school teacher in the nearby village, often has to work as a full-time homemaker and a full-time teacher. While the clothes were washing, I stepped onto the balcony, letting the cool morning breeze brush against my face as I hung the clothes to dry. Suddenly, I felt a sharp pain and cramps in my stomach—I realised my periods had started, what a finish to the trip, I wondered. I then decided to take a bath, letting the warm water soothe my aching muscles and cramps. When I emerged, the comforting aroma of freshly brewed tea greeted me. Raghuvendra had prepared tea, and its warmth helped calm my cramps. It was one of the most amazing milk tea experiences ever. Feeling a bit better, I decided to make onion parathas and tomato *chutney*. The kitchen was filled with the sizzling sound of the parathas cooking and the tangy scent of the *chutney*. Although my parathas turned out a bit hard, it was the first dish I made for Raghuvendra. He jokingly blamed the flour, saying I was perfect. I couldn't help but blush with embarrassment.

We ate the hard-chewy parathas with *chutney* and salad, then rested for a while. The sun streamed in through the windows, casting a warm glow over us as we lounged in the living room. Next, it was time to pack again. I had

126

decided to visit my mom back there in Varanasi. Packing is a task I always dread. At home, my mom would usually do it for me, but now I had to manage it myself, despite the cramps. After packing, it was time for lunch. We made *Kundru* (ivy gourd) *bhujia* with rice and *dal*. Once we finished eating, it was time to leave for our train back to Varanasi. Raghuvendra was excited about surprising his family, as none of them knew about his trip to India.

We arrived at the station, the hustle and bustle of travellers around us, and boarded the train. At the station, I stepped off the train to buy something to eat. The vendors called out their wares, the scent of snacks mingling with the cool air. Once the train departed, we were served water bottles, sandwiches, and tea. Raghuvendra quickly opened his sandwich and started eating, but I wasn't in the mood as it had mayonnaise in it and I disliked it. We chatted for a while about finances, and Raghuvendra explained how starting with small amounts now could significantly multiply with time by the power of compounding. His voice was soothing, and his insights kept me engaged despite the discomfort due to the menstrual cramps.

After a while, around 8 pm, dinner was served. The meal consisted of rice, *roti,* vegetable curry, dal, and pickles. The aroma of the hot food filled the compartment, mingling with the hum of the train's wheels against the tracks. We ate in comfortable silence, savouring the simple yet satisfying meal. After finishing, we went to our seats, which were the side upper and side lower berths. I climbed up to the side upper seat, the gentle rocking of the train lulling me to sleep. In the morning, as the train reached Varanasi, I felt a wave of relief wash over me—our secret trip had finally come to an end.

We arrived in Varanasi at 4 am, greeted by the stillness of the early morning. We decided to go out for tea, seeking the warmth and comfort of a hot beverage. The vendor handed us steaming cups of Kulhad tea, the earthy scent of the clay cups enhancing the tea's flavour. I sipped it slowly, enjoying every bit of the tea I love so much. While enjoying the tea he teased, "You didn't ask any questions—the ones we discussed before the trip."

I had forgotten our plan to ask each other questions to know each other better. I quickly retrieved my diary where I had written down a few questions. We sat beside each other under the shade in the station. I looked into his eyes and asked, "At first, you were confused about us being suitable partners. What made you rethink and give it one more try? What do you think about us now?"

Raghuvendra's eyes softened as he pondered the question, the early morning light casting a gentle glow on his face. He took a deep breath and began to share his thoughts, his words thoughtful and sincere.

Raghuvendra:

I've experienced a lot of pain in love, going through a roller coaster of emotions. It wasn't because my ex cheated or that I wasn't good enough. We just didn't have the courage to face the uncertainties together. We could have blamed each other, but in truth, we both did our best with the wisdom we had at the time. Eventually, we mutually decided to part ways. Moving on wasn't easy, but I believe new love stories are possible if we're open and willing to heal.

When I met you in Varanasi, I noticed you weren't opening up, and you kept your emotions inside. It made me think about how hard it must have been for you, lacking the support of your father, especially when pressured into marriage. At first, you spoke superficially, not expressing opinions or vision about life or relationships, and I felt angry. I thought you had surrendered to family pressure.

Over time, I stopped judging you and began to understand your situation. I developed deep empathy for you but realized that hiding my feelings about my ex could lead to cruelty. My friend, Lekshmi, advised me to be honest with you, warning that marrying without fully accepting you would cause suffering for both of us. So, I opened up to you, and your calm, non-judgmental response brought me relief. In the span of those two months when we didn't talk, I realised you showed great patience, and over time, I started to feel a connection with you. After two months of that small interaction, I somehow enjoyed talking to you, getting a feeling of talking to some old friend. At first, I wasn't even attracted to you in a romantic way, which worried me, but as time passed, my wounds healed, and we grew closer.

I admire your judgement-free nature and simplicity, and that's why I decided to give our relationship a chance.

I value a simple, grounded lifestyle, and seeing how excited you were about my plan to settle in a village and contribute to the community strengthened my decision. Even though you may not always know how to support me, I feel your sincerity and willingness to walk this journey together."

Though I had heard bits and pieces of his thoughts and inner struggles before, listening to Raghuvendra's full account was different. I found myself enjoying the way he described everything in detail. So, I kept listening, occasionally responding with a simple, "Hmmmm," letting him continue.

Raghuvendra:

I've always wanted to do something for others, not just focus on having kids, taking care of family, making money, and then fading away in an ordinary life. The sense of being useful gives me the joy of living. Many girls wouldn't want to sacrifice or support their husband in such unconventional quests—they'd prefer a comfortable life, making money, and enjoying material things. But you're different. You genuinely want to contribute to something greater, even if your motivation sometimes fluctuates.

I also shared my concerns about my ageing parents with you, and I felt that you're a good human being who can bring everyone together as a family. I truly value your sincerity in being such a supportive partner. Why I gave our relationship a try is a complex question to answer, and I could go on talking about it, but it boils down to the fact that you've shown me many traits of partnership I've always hoped for.

Interestingly, everyone who knew about my past relationship supported my decision to be with you. During our trip to Nepal, even Prerna was impressed by your simplicity and friendliness. And now, here we are, sitting at the railway station, talking about things we never imagined we'd discuss."

The station around us buzzed with the quiet activities of early risers and travellers, but in that moment, it felt like it was just the two of us, wrapped in our own little bubble of conversations.

I nodded thoughtfully at Raghuvendra's reply, and he turned the question back to me, "What about you? Why did you stick around even after all the confusion, and me giving you a perception of an emotionally unstable man?"

I took a moment to gather my thoughts and replied, "When we first started talking, I was really mindful of all the societal norms a girl is taught from childhood. I didn't open up to you completely. But right from the beginning, the way you suggested things about my studies made me see you as a responsible person. I was already attracted to you for that—seeing a responsible man with strong family values. What more had I expected from an arranged marriage? I admired how you planned to take care of your elderly parents. Even though you had your doubts, I genuinely respected your honesty. It must have been tough for you to confess all those things after months of talking. I deeply value honesty in a man because it was something my previous relationship lacked. My ex cheated on me, leaving me with so many unanswered questions. Even after your confession, you were willing to face me and answer all my questions.

That evening, after you shared everything with me, I couldn't sleep. My mind raced with thoughts about the impact of ending the engagement or going forward with a marriage that lacked love—for both me and my family. I even wondered if it might be an excuse for you to create distance between us. These negative thoughts lingered for several nights, filling me with confusion. Eventually, I realised that we both needed clarity; that's when I decided to take a break, allowing myself to rediscover my goals and giving you space to find emotional stability.

Just months before, I had experienced similar feelings, so I understood the turmoil. This realisation encouraged me to stay patient, to give us both time to understand each other more profoundly.

I never felt like stopping our conversations, once we started, I could find that stability and a good friend vibe which I missed in the initial months of our conversation. As our conversation continued, I was more amazed by your decision to move back to a small place, take care of both your parents and children, and do something meaningful for society. I felt like praising you, not just as a partner, but also as a person. Looking back now, I feel like we've really explored who we are. Even during the days when I gave you the silent treatment, waiting for you to text first, you were the one who broke the ice asking about some random stuff. All I can say is that we both chose to take a chance to know better without giving up on each other. And look here we are."

Raghuvendra nodded in agreement, a thoughtful expression on his face.

My next question was, "Do you think you've moved on from your ex? Do you still have contact with her?"

He hesitated before answering, "I actually don't know what moving on really means."

I explained what it meant for me, "Moving on means accepting that there's no future together and being ready to go separate ways."

He then replied, "I haven't had contact with her for a long time, but recently one of my friends mentioned she wanted to talk about some things since we used to share an apartment. She had contacted me twice and she had the idea about this trip."

Hearing this made me feel a pang of hurt. I knew they were in contact, but I had no idea about their closeness or that she knew about our trip, which turned into a misconception to me. I got confused with the word trip. What Raghuvendra meant was a trip to India and what I got was our trip to Nepal. As we talked, my emotions were a whirl-wind. Part of me felt reassured by his honesty and our shared understanding, while another part of me felt a lingering unease. The depth of our conversation highlighted the trust we were building, but also the vulnerabilities we both carried. We continued talking about various topics, like how his parents introduced him to a girl, and after a week of talking, he realised she was very different and not suitable for him.

Before we knew it, the train had arrived. It was time to say goodbye. Raghuvendra found his seat in the local train, put his stuff down, and came back out to talk a bit more. Finally, the train signalled its departure. We shook hands, as Raghuvendra noted that hugging wasn't appropriate at this place as the society is still not fully open to opposite genders hugging in public. Standing there on the platform, my heart ached with a mixture of sadness and hope. As the train pulled away, it was a bittersweet moment. We weren't sure if this was a final goodbye or just a temporary one, but it was definitely time for a heartfelt farewell.

Watching the train disappear into the distance, I felt a surge of emotions—relief that our secret trip was over, sadness at parting ways, and a lingering uncertainty about what the future held. The journey back to Varanasi had been more than just a physical trip; it was a journey through our feelings, our pasts, and our hopes for the future.

10. Acceptance

In our tradition, the eldest brother is expected to take on the role of a father or share responsibilities with the father in caring for their siblings. But greed erodes the values and ethics in most of the people.

The sound of my phone broke through the silence of the room, pulling me out of a deep sleep. It was 9 AM, and Raghuvendra was calling.

Groggily, I answered, "Hello..."

Raghuvendra's playful voice came through, "Look at you, still sleeping while I'm already working in the kitchen. Your uncle is coming to meet me."

I felt a mix of shock and happiness. We hadn't discussed anything formal about marriage yet, or we didn't feel the need to do so. We had accepted each other without saying anything directly.

I had earlier asked him, "What do you feel about us?"

He had replied sincerely, "I'm not sure, but I feel really nice when I see our photos together. It's more than friendship."

Raghuvendra updated me on everything happening there. I think it is his way to speak through actions. And he updated me about my uncle being at his home, spoke volume about our relationship sliding towards an alliance of hearts. He told me my uncle was in a very jolly mood that day and even entered the kitchen where everyone was working. It's not common for male guests, especially from the bride's family, to enter the kitchen. My uncle joked, "I don't know how to cook well, but my brothers do. They often cook."

After my father passed away in a road accident, my uncles stepped in as our guardian. My father, being the eldest among his siblings, was often remembered fondly by my grandmother. She used to say, "Your father was dark in complexion, but his face always had a glow, making him the most handsome of all my sons. In our tradition, the eldest brother is expected to take on the role of a father or share responsibilities with the father in caring for their siblings. Elder sisters, on the other hand, are expected to be motherly but are not obligated to care for their younger siblings after they get married and move to their husband's house.

My dad passed away when I was just six, I don't have many memories of him. But I've never forgotten the moments when a father's presence was deeply missed. I remember school's parent-teacher meetings, watching my mom sit alone while other kids had both their parents by their side. I saw her struggle—searching for a trusted relative to lean on for important decisions, waiting in long lines for cooking gas, or silently worrying about our future. I witnessed her break under the weight of it all, tears slipping quietly when she thought no one was watching. The hardest part, though, was learning about my eldest uncle, who had always been like a guardian angel, borrowing a large sum of money from my mom and never returning it. That money was her safety net, meant to protect us from hard times and help with weddings, but he left us in financial distress. My mom, bound by family ties, couldn't fight back. To the world, my uncle seemed like a great brother and caring uncle, but I learned the harsh truth: greed can overpower even the strongest bonds of family. That's the reality of the world we live in.

Now that I'm grown, and my mom shares more with me, I've come to see the masks people wear. My whole childhood, I was led to believe that my family was the best in the world. In a way, that illusion gave me a normal, happy childhood, and for that, I'm grateful. My mom shielded me from the harsh truths, and while it was all a trick of sorts, I appreciate every ounce of her effort.

From her, I also learned the value of forgiveness. She never harboured grudges or ill-will towards my uncle or anyone else. In my eyes, she remains one of the funniest and most cheerful people I've ever known. Her quick wit and infectious laughter bring joy to everyone around her. She is my best friend, a wonderful teacher, and a bundle of love. Oh, and yes—she's a little chubby, too, making her even cuter!

Until a few years ago, arranging marriages for girls wasn't easy. Families had to pay a hefty dowry—a practice that, unfortunately, still persists in many parts of India. In my state, Uttar Pradesh, and neighbouring Bihar, every groom has a price, and those with government jobs fetch the highest demands. Families of brides, wanting the best for their daughters, often prioritise financially secure men. Government employees, especially administrative servants, top the list with the largest dowry demands, followed closely by other officials. Even a simple office worker in a government department can command a significant dowry.

I understand that government jobs are more secure compared to private ones, but they come with limitations in growth and opportunities. Despite this, they remain in high demand due to their rarity and stability. Unfortunately, the allure of government jobs often isn't just about honest work—some seek them for the opportunity to engage in corruption, without a cap on personal gain. That's a shame. Others choose government jobs just to live an easier, more comfortable life. In a state that's struggled with poverty and instability for decades, securing a government job can seem like a ticket to breaking the generational cycle of hardship. But it's unsustainable, and this mindset isn't steering society in a better direction.

What's especially ironic is that boys in prestigious roles like the Indian Administrative Services (IAS) or Indian Police Services (IPS)—positions meant to fight social injustices—often demand the highest dowries.

I'm incredibly grateful that Raghuvendra's family is truly against dowry, and Raghuvendra himself shares that belief. He's even expressed a desire for a simple wedding, saying a temple ceremony with just a few family members would be perfect, provided I agree. We've discussed the dowry system many times, and Raghuvendra points out that it stems from societal ignorance. Many families still save money for their daughters' marriages rather than investing in their education or careers. Meanwhile, boys are pushed to work hard to secure good jobs, knowing that no family will want to marry their daughter to someone unemployed or struggling financially. But the reverse isn't true. A boy is often willing to marry a girl solely based on her looks or the dowry her family can offer.

It's a sad irony. In modern times, women are still objectified, with their beauty and bodies seen as their most valuable assets. If a girl doesn't meet societal standards of beauty—fair skin, tall stature, delicate features—a higher dowry often compensates. Some girls, too, prefer marrying well-settled men so they can stay at home and avoid the challenges of working outside. And yes, there are a few who misuse their looks to gain favours at work. This saddens me, as it perpetuates the harmful notion that a woman's body and beauty can be traded for anything.

Girls need to understand that their lives shouldn't revolve around beauty or seeking attention. They should focus on their education, careers, hobbies, sports, and learning skills that enrich their lives. Raghuvendra feels strongly about this too—he believes that the mistreatment and social issues women face will only disappear when they are empowered, when they build their own futures and reject the trap of a beauty-centred life.

After my uncle left, Raghuvendra shared their conversation about our marriage. My uncle had asked him about possible wedding dates, and Raghuvendra mentioned his plan to come in February for the ceremony. I quickly counted the months—it was already November, and the wedding was just three months away. It felt so soon, especially considering how long it had taken for us to truly accept each other. The thought of such a big life change happening so quickly overwhelmed me.

Later that evening, my mom called. She told me that uncle praised Raghuvendra's manners and graceful personality, but she also expressed concern about what would happen after the wedding. Would Raghuvendra take me with him right away, or would he suggest I stay in the village? In some families, the in-laws can be overbearing, even oppressive, sometimes limiting the bride's freedom to do anything beyond household chores. Although rare nowadays, these situations still exist. In traditional Indian society, parents worry deeply about their daughters' well-being after marriage. They often spend a significant portion of their life savings, sometimes even take on loans, to ensure their daughters marry comfortably. Lavish weddings and dowries are seen as ways to secure a daughter's future. Moreover, my mother, being a single parent, often worried about my future. At times, she would share stories about her own early marriage, where my father was her sole pillar of support. She reminded me of the challenges she faced and how deeply she hoped that I'd find a partner who would stand by me, not only as a spouse but as a true friend. Knowing this, I often felt her concerns more intensely; I understood that her hopes for me stemmed from her own life experiences and the resilience she built on her journey.

I reassured my mom about Raghuvendra's plans for us to live together after marriage and assured him that even if we returned to the village, it would be our decision. She advised me to speak up if anything didn't feel right, and I agreed.

In the end, I was just happy that Raghuvendra and I were on the same path, moving toward becoming life partners and building a family together. Everything was falling into place.

Days passed quickly, and soon Raghuvendra had to catch his flight back to New Delhi, and then to Germany. He came a day earlier from his village to spend time with his relatives in Delhi. I was already back in Delhi, so we decided to meet up again while he was in the city, this time not secretly but with the knowledge of our family. Since my cooking went bad during our last meeting, I decided to treat him with hand cooked mushroom chilli and fresh parathas.

The day before, I made a list of ingredients and went shopping to ensure everything was perfect. The next morning, I woke up early, cleaned my room, arranged everything neatly, made my bed, and headed to the kitchen. I prepared the mushroom chilli and dough, planning to serve him fresh, hot parathas when he arrived.

I had already booked Raghuvendra's train ticket to arrive in the morning so we could spend more time together before he headed off to visit his relatives in the evening. But traffic was awful that day, and I was late—he ended up waiting almost 30 minutes at the railway station. I felt terrible and rushed to pick him up. When I finally arrived, he greeted me with his usual calm smile, and all my stress melted away.

As we drove, Raghuvendra mentioned that his aunt—his mother's sister—had invited us over. He suggested we could visit her first and then find some time later to spend together. I liked the plan and agreed. On the way to his aunt's, we stopped to buy chocolates for her grandchildren and some fresh fruits for everyone. When we arrived, his aunt greeted us with such warmth that I immediately felt at home. Raghuvendra handed out the gifts he had brought, and the kids' faces lit up with excitement. They were so happy, and just because I handed the gifts over to them, they quickly made me their favourite! It was heartwarming to see their innocence and playful energy.

We all chatted for a while, enjoyed a lovely lunch, and rested a bit before heading back to my place. It was a simple day, but moments like these made me appreciate the beauty of everyday life with Raghuvendra.

When we reached my apartment, Raghuvendra wasn't feeling well—he had a headache and some gas trouble, probably due to the hot weather and all the travelling. After he rested for a bit, I offered him some mushroom chilli that I had made. He tried it, gave me a few suggestions to improve it, but overall, he liked it (how could he not? I made it with a lot of love). I packed the rest for him to have later for dinner and let him rest peacefully for a while.

He woke up around 6:30 PM and suggested we go out somewhere. I proposed visiting the nearby ISKCON temple, and Raghuvendra happily agreed. We booked a cab to the ISKCON Temple in Dwarka, Delhi. Once we arrived, we had *darshan* (offering prayers), then sat down in the corridor in front of the temple. The peacefulness of the place was soothing, and we began chatting. Raghuvendra shared memories of his time in Varanasi, when he was preparing for the engineering entrance exam. He recounted the funny and challenging moments of his bachelor life, like living with his friend Saquib, pretending he was Hindu to rent a place, and surviving on simple meals like khichdi and bananas. I laughed when he told me about going home without any luggage, stuffing only his undergarments in his pockets, just to travel light.

After praying, we walked around the temple grounds and found a balcony facing the main road. We took some selfies, capturing the serene atmosphere, and realised it was already 8 PM. Raghuvendra then mentioned he was craving *Litti* (a traditional dish from Bihar, UP and Jharkhand states of made from spiced black gram powder stuffed in balls made from whole wheat flour cooked over open flame, mainly coal/charcoal) *Chokha* (mashed vegetable), a famous dish from Bihar and Uttar Pradesh. We headed to a place known for its authentic *Litti-Chokha* after stopping for tea. The meal was delicious, and it felt so heartwarming to see Raghuvendra enjoying it. Despite my initial impression of him being sophisticated due to his work abroad, I was happy to discover his simplicity and down-to-earth nature. I even clicked a picture of him holding his plate, grinning ear to ear—it was such a joyful moment.

We walked through the streets afterward, enjoying the cool night breeze. By the time we checked the clock, it was already 10 PM. Raghuvendra's mom called, reminding him that it was late and that he should ensure I got home safely before heading to his aunt's place. What I truly admire about Raghuvendra's family is how easily they've accepted me, which is rare in Indian families.

They always make me feel valued and cared for, and it's a comforting feeling.

When we got close to his aunt's house, I told Raghuvendra he could head home since my apartment was still far, and it was late. But he insisted on dropping me off, well aware of the safety concerns women face, especially at night. Sometimes I feel overwhelmed by how unsafe society has become for women—it's disheartening that an entire gender often feels vulnerable when alone at night. Realising his concern was valid, I let him drop me off.

Once we reached my apartment, we hugged, and Raghuvendra headed back to his aunt's place. I went inside, freshened up, and reflected on the day. It had been a beautiful, well-spent day with Raghuvendra and his family.

That night, sleep eluded me as I found myself missing Raghuvendra already. The reality of him leaving for Germany the next morning weighed heavily on my mind. I insisted on going to the airport with him, and he agreed, grateful for my presence.

That morning, I got ready in a kurti and leggings, completing my look with a small black Bindi. I knew how much Raghuvendra liked it; he often commented on how beautiful girls looked in Indian attire, especially with Bindis and Jhumkas.

When I reached his aunt's place, Raghuvendra was busy packing. I reminded him to double-check that he hadn't forgotten anything. I handed him the letter which captured my feelings and suggested him to read later. On the front of the envelope, I wrote, "This is the last letter I am sending you as your fiancée, as we will soon be husband and wife." Inside, I expressed how much I cherished the care I felt during our trip to Nepal, recognizing the genuine and caring man behind the conversations we had over the months. I wished him luck as he transitioned from Germany to Sweden, reflecting on how our meeting in Delhi felt different now that we were certain about our future together. I pondered the purpose of our trip—though I still couldn't fully understand it, I sensed we were both navigating fears about each other and our future.

His cousin's wife arrived just after dropping her kids off at school. We hadn't had much time to chat the other day, and today was no different, as I had to head to the airport.

At the airport, we took a few pictures together before he went inside for the security check. It was bittersweet, capturing those moments knowing they might be our last for a while. On my way back, his aunt invited me for tea. After some light chit-chat, I finally got to have a soulful conversation with his cousin's wife. We shared stories and laughter, which felt comforting after the emotional morning.

After an hour, I thanked them for their warmth and love and made my way back to my apartment. Once inside, I laid on my bed, reflecting on the journey we had taken together. We had started the trip feeling unsure about each other—though "fully unsure" wouldn't quite capture it. It was more about embracing our in-person vibe and letting things unfold naturally. Now, everything felt so clear; there was no longer any emotional turbulence or doubt within me about us being together. It all just made sense. The trip made sense.

In that quiet moment, I felt grateful for every experience we shared and excited for what lay ahead.

11. The Unseen Layers

As we learn and grow, our thoughts evolve, and the past becomes a neglected history as we build a beautiful future, working in the present.

After the trip, our love began to blossom in ways I hadn't imagined. We grew closer, our conversations naturally drifting toward a shared future. We started discussing our lives together, imagining our wedding, and making plans for the days ahead. It felt like we were building something beautiful, brick by brick.

A few weeks later, it was time for me to head home for a month. The Diwali and *Chhath* (an ancient Hindu festival dedicated to the Sun God (*Surya*) and his wife *Usha*, primarily celebrated in the Indian states of Bihar, Jharkhand, Uttar Pradesh, and the Terai region of Nepal) were approaching, and I was also looking forward to attending my childhood school friend's wedding. I was excited—it would be the first time I'd see them since our school days, and I couldn't wait to reconnect.

One day, while Raghuvendra and I were reminiscing about the memories we had already created together, he casually mentioned something about his past with his ex. Though he didn't dwell on it, the comment lingered in my mind, stirring up old doubts. Was he really over her? The question gnawed at me, refusing to be silenced.

During one of our conversations, I couldn't hold it in any longer. "Are you truly ready for marriage?" I asked him, my voice softer than I intended, "Or are you just considering it because it seems like the only option, and you're moving forward because you feel you have to?"

I've always believed in old-school love, the kind where both partners are fully committed, leaving no room for past entanglements. I told him I wouldn't want my husband to be in contact with any of his exes if I wasn't in contact with mine. "If you need more time, take it," I offered, trying to sound understanding but feeling the frustration building inside me.

The situation was made even more complicated by something that had happened the day before. A friend had mentioned she'd spoken with my ex recently, and he'd been curious about my life. He had even suggested a conference call for a casual chat. The suggestion shook me. I didn't want any lingering connections to the past, not even the smallest ones. I asked my friend to either block me or him—anything to cut ties completely.

I remember a conversation with my mom vividly, one that took place after she had met his mother in Delhi. We had discussed the uncertainties I was feeling, and naturally, she was concerned. One day, she gently brought up the topic again, asking if everything was going well between us. Her voice carried a quiet worry, and she made sure to ask if I had agreed to the marriage under any kind of family pressure.

What struck me was the gradual, yet firm, way she asked me if I was sure about my decision. She said something that stayed with me: "You can still back out, even if 1% of doubt or pressure is lingering in your mind." Her words were filled with both wisdom and care. She reminded me that no societal expectations or norms would stand by me if I were to end up living an unhappy married life.

Her concern wasn't about what people might say, but about my happiness and well-being. She made it clear that no marriage is worth it if it costs your peace of mind, and it was a subtle yet powerful reminder that I should make decisions for myself, not because of others. It was one of those moments that made me reflect deeply on what I truly wanted.

So, when Raghuvendra spoke about his ex, it struck a chord deep within me, one that resonated with the uncertainty and fear I was trying so hard to leave behind.

I was relieved when Raghuvendra, understanding my concerns, reassured me that marrying me wasn't just an option for him—it was what he truly wanted. Yet, I felt it would be wise to give us a bit more time to fully embrace the reality of marriage. The trip, our deepening connection, and his meeting with my uncle to finalise the wedding dates—it all felt overwhelming, especially after months of uncertainty. Sometimes, the mind struggles to process so much at once. I had always craved a clear answer, and now that I had it, I found it difficult to accept it all at once.

Amidst these emotional tides, I also had to prepare all the necessary documents for my new job. Life became a whirlwind of planned schedules and responsibilities. Raghuvendra, too, was busy. He had to join his new job in Sweden and was preoccupied with packing, shifting, and saying goodbye to friends in Germany. Despite our hectic routines, we kept each other updated with pictures, sharing glimpses of our day-to-day lives. Even when life pulled us in different directions, we stayed anchored in each other.

One thing became clear to me during this time: we weren't the type to shy away from uncomfortable conversations. It was one of the reasons we held on to each other—we faced those tough talks, even when it was hard for both of us. But confronting them, reflecting on them, led to some of our most beautiful memories. And here we are now, sharing our story.

Every couple has their own shortcomings, and it's up to them how they handle them. You have to go through discomfort to find comfort, especially when there's some lingering baggage from the past. But we did that, and it brought us closer, shaping the path we're now walking together.

As the days slipped by, I finally returned to Delhi after attending all the functions. A mix of excitement and nervousness swirling within me as I prepared to start my first job. It was December 18th, the official joining day, with instructions to report by the 30th. I had been posted to Jaunpur, a small city about 68 kilometres from Varanasi. The responsibility of managing everything on my own—from the move to settling into a new place— felt daunting. Thankfully, my cousin Avinash and my uncle stepped in to help with the shift from Delhi to Jaunpur. I probably drove Avinash crazy with my constant instructions and elder-sister tantrums, but he handled it all with patience.

In the chaos of packing, unpacking, and adjusting to a new environment, I became so busy that Raghuvendra and I barely had time to talk. Moving in with new housemates added to my discomfort, making it harder to open up as freely as before. During one of our rare conversations, Raghuvendra noticed the growing distance and gently pointed out, "We haven't been talking much since you moved." His words struck a chord, and I realised just how true they were. It's so easy to get swept away by the demands of work and the hectic pace of professional life. But his words also brought me a sense of reassurance— my presence in his life mattered enough for him to notice the lack of conversations and to express it, even if it was just a polite complaint. It was his way of showing that he missed our connection and valued the bond we shared.

Not long after, I caught a cold and lost my voice, making communication even more challenging. When I finally managed to speak to Raghuvendra, he teased me, "Oh, finally, I can have some peace." His light heartedness brought a smile to my face, despite the discomfort.

As I gradually settled into my new routine— exercising, working, and studying—things began to feel more balanced. Our conversations became regular again, and with each one, I could see Raghuvendra's love for me as clearly as he could see mine. The initial distance had faded, replaced by a deeper understanding and connection. Even through the ups and downs, our bond remained strong, a testament to the love we were building together.

My role as a program coordinator at the NGO is focused on rural literacy. One of my most memorable moments from the past few months of work is meeting a 16-17-year-old boy named Shyam. His mother worked as a maid, and despite their limited means, Shyam had a vision and drive that truly inspired me. He had created a robotic car, inspired by a remote-control car he had once seen with the son of the man his mother worked for.

Shyam told me about his dream of becoming a robotics engineer and how toys he couldn't afford had sparked his desire to ensure no child would experience the same limitations. Unfortunately, preparing for engineering colleges like IIT is expensive in India, and our NGO's resources were already stretched. I was disappointed that we couldn't support him financially.

I shared Shyam's story with Raghuvendra, and he immediately offered to teach Shyam physics for IIT entrance, while I volunteered to teach him chemistry. As we started helping Shyam, it felt like we both were teaching our child together. Shyam's happiness and gratitude were overwhelming, and it was clear that he was a brilliant student with immense potential. Moments like these made the work deeply fulfilling and brought a unique sense of connection between Raghu and me.

During those first three months, when my salary hadn't yet been credited to my account, Raghuvendra supported me financially without even asking for it. He even surprised me with a new phone, knowing I had planned to buy one with my first pay check, saying it was a gift to celebrate my new job. These small but meaningful gestures revealed just how much he truly cared for me.

Raghuvendra has a keen eye for photography, often sharing stunning pictures of flowers and landscapes with me. They were truly amazing, and I loved using them as backgrounds for the quotes I posted on my Instagram page. Sometimes, I even recorded my voice to accompany the posts. During a difficult time in my life, I created a space where I could express the unsaid words and feelings I had about my ex. Even after our breakup, I continued using that space as an outlet for my deep emotions and the hardships I faced. In some way, I think I was holding onto it because we never had a proper goodbye. Sometimes, I also regretted cutting ties with him without a final farewell. He was never willing to completely let go, and I guess that kept me tethered too.

Last year, when I discovered he had been cheating on me. Despite the betrayal, I initially tried to make things work, clinging to the hope of resolution. But when he put in no effort, I knew it was over. I told him we couldn't continue, that the love and affection we once had were gone, and that it was time to part ways without any unnecessary drama. His reaction, however, caught me off guard. He panicked and became erratic, even threatening me, saying I couldn't imagine the consequences if I left. His behaviour terrified me, especially since my family had already begun preparing my bio-data for marriage as I was nearing the end of my studies. We had made a pact to go our separate ways as friends after securing jobs, but that never worked for me.

When my ex found out about my family's search for a match, he kept reminding me of the dreams we once shared—about marriage and children. I could sense his sadness and regret, as he admitted he never imagined things would spiral so badly. Despite this, I had already begun distancing myself. I stopped sharing details of my life with him, something that was once second nature to me. Noticing this shift, he tried to make an effort to win me back, but it was too late.

One day, overwhelmed with frustration, I sat down with a pen and paper, determined to analyse whether staying in touch with him would ever bring happiness to either of us. After much thought, I realised I couldn't find a single reason to stay connected. I had already made up my mind to move on, and my family was actively searching for a suitable partner. I knew I needed to prepare myself for the changes an arranged marriage would bring, and that wouldn't be possible if I still had feelings for him.

The next morning, I blocked him from everywhere—on social media, messaging apps, and phone calls. We shared a common Gmail account, and when I discovered he was still tracking me through it, I changed all my account details. Fortunately, we didn't have many mutual friends, so cutting ties wasn't too difficult. My close friends, who had long advised me to sever all connections with him, supported me through this tough transition.

Despite everything, I continued to maintain my Instagram page. One day, I shared a quote with Raghuvendra, not realising the impact it would have on him. He was shocked and asked if I still had feelings for my ex. In reality, none of that was true. My recent posts were simply an expression of the insecurities I had been dealing with. However, Raghuvendra misunderstood, and it deeply hurt him. I had only given him a brief mention of my previous relationship, not the full story, which perhaps contributed to his insecurity.

Raghuvendra was so upset that he accused me of breaking his trust and not being honest. He told me I was being foolish for continuing with a page that reminded me of a past relationship that ended with my ex cheating on me. In his anger, he said, "Don't be the kind of girl who attracts toxic men and doesn't appreciate good men. I can't be toxic. So, you either choose my kindness or reconsider our relationship."

This incident deeply disturbed me, making me realise that I had unintentionally made Raghuvendra feel the same way I once felt—a situation I had always hoped to avoid. I never intended to keep anything from my past. I was fully prepared to be Raghuvendra's. Despite his hurt, he still stayed on a video call with me until I fell asleep, showing a kindness that I deeply admired. The next day, I reassured Raghuvendra of my full commitment to our relationship, with no lingering feelings that could cause insecurity. I chose to be completely honest with him, reaffirming my dedication to our future together.

I deleted all the sad quotes and reflections from my page because, to me, they were old, decayed leaves that needed to be discarded to make way for new growth. I realised that we humans are so complex emotionally that we often don't understand what goes on in our heads. Even worse, we sometimes manipulate and trick ourselves. But time is the greatest teacher. As we learn and grow, our thoughts evolve, and the past becomes a neglected history as we build a beautiful future, working in the present.

As days went by, I adhered to my routine of diet, exercise, and daily tasks, with Raghuvendra as my accountability partner. He shared valuable insights about health and fitness, often drawn from his reading of the latest research in the field. My mornings usually began with curd and oats, followed by preparing lunch to take to the office. For evening snacks, I enjoyed milk tea without sugar, and dinner was a simple affair. This regular routine was reflected in the shine on my face and the fitness of my body.

As New Year's approached, Raghuvendra would often show me the snowfall outside his window, taking selfies with me on video calls. Despite the miles between us, I could still feel the warmth and growing closeness we shared through the cold weather. On New Year's Eve, my roommate and I decided to make a homemade cake with *rawa/suji* (semolina), garnished with dry fruits. Raghuvendra guided me through the process virtually, and once the cake was ready, we all took selfies together—me, Neha, and Raghuvendra on the other side of the world—wishing each other a happy new year.

Reflecting on 2023, I realised what an eventful year it had been. January brought Raghuvendra into my life and awarded me my master's degree. February witnessed my roka ceremony and my move to Delhi. March was filled with the joy of Holi (the vibrant and deeply significant

Hindu festival known as the Festival of Colours, Love, and Spring) celebrations, which I had thought would be my last Holi before marriage, though it turned out otherwise. April arrived with the first gifts from Raghu while May, my birthday month was a mix of great joy and some disappointment. June was a time of ups and downs, while July tested my resilience like never before. But by August, I emerged as a stronger, more emotionally independent version of myself and my confidence-boosting job interview. September marked the deepening of my relationship with Raghuvendra. October gifted me with a trip to Pokhara and the joy of passing my interview. November flew by with the festive hustle of Diwali, followed by Chhath, and ended with a friend's wedding. December marked the beginning of a new chapter as I joined my job and moved to Jaunpur. Coincidentally, both his parents and I were posted in the same district, Jaunpur.

Wow! What a year it had been—so full of events, growth, and milestones. It was a year of meaningful progress, both emotionally and professionally, and I ended it with the gifts of a new job and my lifelong partner.

12. Reflection

*But the truth is, we often find strength we didn't know
we had, and in the end, reality rarely matches the terrors
we conjure in our minds.*

On the first day of 2024, I began by expressing deep gratitude to God for the year just passed, filled with cherished memories and hard-earned lessons. There had been challenging days—days that tested my patience and resolve—but now, I could see those trials as moments of growth and resilience. That morning, I headed to the office. It was my first day at work. Our office had organised a gathering for the staff, their families, and alumni from our NGO. Even the founder, Mrs. Gayathri, joined us for the celebration. The event began with a worship ceremony, followed by activities for the children we support, and concluded with a shared lunch that brought everyone together.

After the event, a group of us went to a cosy restaurant nearby, carrying the warmth of the day's camaraderie with us. As we made our way there, I was on the phone with Raghuvendra, sharing the day's details, laughing about the kids' antics, and painting little scenes for him to imagine. When the food arrived, I hastily promised to call him later to wish him a goodnight and ended the call. This ritual has become a comforting part of our daily routine, a simple but meaningful way to stay close, no matter the distance.

But as the day continued, I got wrapped up with new friends and lively conversations. Caught in the spirit of the moment, I completely forgot to call him back or send my usual goodnight message. Only later did I realise that, on the first day of the year, I had let Raghuvendra fall asleep without our familiar, reassuring exchange. It felt like a small slip, yet it weighed on me. These seemingly minor gestures—keeping promises, prioritising one another—lay the foundation of a relationship. Raghuvendra, even on his busiest days, always made sure to prioritise me, a quiet but unwavering commitment that made me reflect on my own actions. And in that reflection, I resolved to nurture what we shared with the same care he had always shown me.

Psychological evidence suggests that small, consistent expressions of love and care play a pivotal role in sustaining healthy, long-lasting relationships. When we overlook these simple rituals, even unintentionally, it can foster feelings of neglect that linger beneath the surface. In my case, it wasn't that Raghuvendra wasn't a priority; it was simply a moment of distraction that led me to forget the familiar comfort of sending him a goodnight message. A simple text or a quick goodbye on the call could have kept that thread of connection intact. I'm learning that clear communication is more than just a habit—it's the foundation of lasting love.

This experience has reinforced the importance of practising gratitude and mindfulness, especially within relationships. It's all too easy to let the small things slip, especially as time passes. But I'm beginning to see that regularly showing affection and prioritising those we care about, even in seemingly minor ways, is essential. Many relationships don't end with dramatic conflict; instead, they often erode slowly, the result of unspoken expectations, neglect, or the failure to grow together. Often, these symptoms are overlooked, mistaken for laziness or simple routine. Raghuvendra brought it up in passing, laughing that he'd gone to sleep without our nightly ritual. I felt a wave of guilt, but I was also grateful for the reminder.

During college, I often saw relationships that felt imbalanced—where one partner was overly demanding while the other compromised for the sake of physical attraction or the thrill of the moment. I struggled to understand such dynamics. Love, like friendship, must be a two-way street. Real love thrives on mutual respect, shared growth, and an exchange of care that goes both ways. Anything less risks creating a lopsided companionship, one that doesn't withstand life's inevitable challenges.

Looking ahead, I am more committed than ever to ensuring my actions genuinely reflect my feelings for Raghuvendra. I want him to always feel just how much he means to me, through every small gesture and shared moment. In this way, I hope to nurture a love that is both balanced and deeply fulfilling, a true partnership built on presence, care, and mutual growth.

Since Raghuvendra and I had grown comfortable enough to show each other our quirkiest, silliest sides on video calls, it had become a ritual to pull ridiculous faces, flashing exaggerated grins, and laughing at each other's absurdity. One evening, during one of these playful exchanges, Raghuvendra leaned closer to the camera, squinting with mock seriousness. He pointed out, with a teasing glint, that the gap between my front teeth had widened. I had noticed it too, but true to form, I'd brushed it aside. Yet, when he mentioned it, it somehow felt different—like I couldn't ignore it any longer. The last thing I wanted was a "window" between my teeth.

It wasn't just the gap. I had a few cavities as well, a result of my lifelong sweet tooth and my careless childhood habit of dozing off with chocolates still tucked in my mouth. It's funny how childhood habits have a way of catching up with us. And it's not just about candy; it's a reminder of how poor health habits, often unconsciously encouraged by parents out of love or lack of awareness, leave lasting impacts. Many parents, either too controlling or too busy, miss the chance to build healthy routines with their kids. It makes me wish that healthy parenting practices, especially around nutrition and habits, were more widely understood.

When Raghuvendra gently suggested me to see a dentist, he mentioned Dr. Saket, an old friend he'd recently reconnected with on Fakebook. With the casual mention that I was his fiancée, Raghuvendra secured me an appointment. When I met Dr. Saket, he examined my teeth with a practised eye, uncovering more issues than I'd anticipated. Three wisdom teeth were in terrible shape, and one molar was swollen and sore. He recommended a root canal for the molar, but my mind fixated on the gap between my front teeth. Like so many of us, I was more concerned with aesthetics than the underlying issues. Besides, I had heard enough horror stories about root canals to dread the thought of one.

Later, I reached out to Suruchi Di, one of my closest friends, who had recently undergone a root canal. She recounted in vivid detail the pain, the days of barely being able to eat, each meal a struggle. Her story fuelled my fears. Raghuvendra, too, shared tales from friends who'd endured the ordeal, reinforcing my dread of the procedure. So, instead of facing my fear head-on, I opted for braces. At first, they felt foreign, cumbersome, like an intruder in my mouth. But eventually, I adjusted, the discomfort becoming a small, manageable inconvenience.

Yet my molar had other plans. The dull ache became a persistent throb, forcing me to confront the inevitable. I braced myself and scheduled the root canal. The experience was intense. I remember the sharp prick of needles, the unpleasant sight of blood, and the strange sensations that coursed through me. The first session was surprisingly easy, thanks to the numbing agent, but the following treatments were a raw experience, no numbing—just the procedure in its pure form. Remarkably, it was manageable, far from the torture I'd expected.

But as life would have it, complications arose. An infection set in, swelling my gums and making another root canal necessary. This time, the pain was bearable, but the medicine tasted vile, like something conjured from a nightmare. Even then, the ordeal was short-lived. With some medication, I was back to normal in no time and didn't even miss a meal because of the pain.

In hindsight, I realised how needlessly I let fear rule my decisions. The dread that I'd built up, fuelled by others' experiences, was greater than the reality itself. It's so easy to let ourselves be haunted by stories we've heard, to let them dictate our expectations. But facing this fear reminded me of our inner resilience, the strength we rarely acknowledge. Reality, it turns out, is often far less frightening than the monsters we imagine.

Time seemed to slip away, and before I knew it, February had arrived. Raghuvendra was supposed to come back to India and marry me. But he got stuck with his new role in Sweden, postponing our wedding to June or later. On the auspicious day of Shivaratri, I found myself reflecting on the year that had passed since our Roka ceremony. The journey with Raghuvendra has been a tapestry woven with both joys and challenges, and I know this pattern will continue throughout our lives. What truly matters, though, is having a partner who stands by you through every high and low, ready to hold your hand when the road gets rough.

That day, the universe had a delightful surprise in store for me—my pending salary was finally credited to my account. This was no ordinary salary; it was my very first, something I had always dreamt of. For years, I had envisioned using my first earnings to spread happiness among my loved ones, and now the moment had come. With a heart full of joy, I decided to buy clothes for everyone in my family for Holi. I managed to fulfil that dream, selecting clothes for each one of my loved ones. The joy I felt was immense, but it was seeing the happiness and satisfaction on my uncle's face that filled me with a deep sense of contentment.

As March arrived, I travelled to my village to celebrate *Holi*. After the wedding, I don't know where I would be staying with Raghavendra, so I wanted to make it my best Holi with mom and my cousins. Holi is a vibrant and deeply significant Hindu festival known as the Festival of Colours, Love, and Spring. There's a unique purity and simplicity to Holi in the village—no showmanship, just genuine joy and heartfelt traditions. The celebration begins with *Holika Dahan*, where a bonfire is lit to symbolise the victory of good over evil. The legend of Holika, the sister of Hiranyakashipu, who was granted a boon to be invulnerable to fire, always comes to mind. She tried to kill her devout nephew, Prahlada, by placing him on her lap in the bonfire, but in a miraculous turn, she was consumed by the flames while Prahlada was saved. This ritual always serves as a poignant reminder of the power of faith and the triumph of goodness.

The day of Holi began with worship, followed by the playful and joyful tradition of throwing colours. In the village, the celebration feels especially pure, with homemade snacks and sweets prepared with love and a sense of community that fills the air. The lush green fields seem to come alive with the spirit of the festival. As the day progressed, we bowed to our elders with *abeer/gulal* (brightly coloured powder) seeking their blessings and offering them dry fruits—a simple gesture that carries so much meaning. The beauty of Holi lies not just in the colours, but in the blessings, the closeness, and the love shared between generations.

As the day ended, my mom gently reminded me that this would be my last Holi with her before I joined my new family next year. Her eyes held a mix of sadness, pride, and love. In that moment, I felt a deep sense of gratitude for the time spent with my family, knowing that these memories would stay with me forever. The festival was not only well spent but also filled with hope and the joy of knowing that no matter where I go, the love and blessings of my family will always be with me. I knew that wherever life takes me, I'll carry the spirit of this Holi with me—spreading happiness and love, just as I did this year.

After returning from the Holi celebration, I quickly got caught up in work, as it was time to finalise the budget plan for the coming year. I spent days and nights gathering data and carefully preparing, ensuring we'd have a sufficient budget to meet our needs. In what felt like the blink of an eye, May arrived—the month of my birthday. Raghuvendra, always thoughtful, had planned ahead and prepared several surprises for me. He gifted me a short yellow cotton kurti, black jeans, and a beautiful pair of sandals, all part of the outfit he requested I wear for the special day. His text arrived exactly at midnight, wishing me a happy birthday, but there was no call as he had a meeting scheduled at the same time. He had mentioned this earlier, perhaps cautious after the previous years' experience when he deliberately didn't call me hahaha.

At midnight, my roommate, Nimmi, surprised me with a delicious cake. Then, Raghuvendra shared a video he had put together, featuring birthday wishes from him and almost all my family members. The video started with him, followed by pictures of my mom and dad, and then messages from my mom, cousins and other family members. It was so touching that I ended up watching it over and over again, tears of joy in my eyes.

Once his meeting was over, Raghuvendra called to wish me a happy birthday and hinted that another gift was waiting for me. He had ordered chocolates and a small, cute wooden memento of us, which I found adorable. It now sits as a cherished showpiece on my table. I started my day with worship, expressing gratitude to God for such a beautiful life, and then there was a celebration at my office, sponsored by my senior. In the evening, we went out for dinner, and everything felt perfect. It was a well-spent birthday, surrounded by my partner and my close ones, making the day truly special.

In the midst of my life starting to be on track, I had already started planning for my next step. I was on the lookout for a career path that would offer me the flexibility to work while still being able to spend quality time with Raghuvendra and, in the future, our children. Unlike others who might prioritise their careers and earnings, I've always believed that the true essence of life lies in the moments we share with our loved ones, our family. Financial stability is crucial, of course, but I can't imagine sacrificing those precious family moments just to climb the corporate ladder. But at the same time, I wanted to be a contributor and a working woman. But I did not know where to start.

Understanding my aspirations, Raghuvendra suggested that I explore a health coaching program. I had already dipped my toes into the coaching world by attending a free course from the International Coaching Association. I've always been someone people feel comfortable opening-up to, sharing their challenges without fear of judgement. I realised that being a good listener, coupled with my understanding of body mechanics, could make me a natural fit for this field.

With the growing prevalence of stressful lifestyle, metabolic disorders and the impact of poor lifestyle choices, the demand for health and wellness coaches is only going to increase. It felt like a calling—a career that aligned perfectly with my values and aspirations. So, I decided to enrol in the course, which cost a significant amount of money. As I had just started earning, it was definitely a big investment for me. Raghuvendra, seeing the financial burden, kindly offered to pay for the course, but I humbly declined. I believed that if I invested my hard-earned money, I would be more driven to make the most of my investment. However, I chose to pay in instalments to manage the expense more comfortably. It was more than just a financial investment; it was an investment in my future, my family, and the countless lives I hope to positively impact. I approached the course with passion and dedication, knowing that it was the key to building a life of balance, flexibility, and meaningful work.

But soon after, I found myself in need of Raghuvendra's help with one of the instalments. In a moment of naivety, I made the mistake of lending all my savings to a senior colleague who expressed a need for financial support. Without thinking it through, I handed over almost all my savings. This senior had been incredibly helpful in guiding me through my job as a newcomer, and out of gratitude, I lent him the money without a second thought. He had promised to return the money the following month, but that promise went unfulfilled.

When I confided in Raghuvendra about what had happened, he was understandably upset. He pointed out that I should have at least sought advice from my mom or someone else who could have guided me wisely before making such a decision. Informing him after lending the money didn't make much sense. I had learned some basics of money management from Raghuvendra, and I failed him by making such an unwise decision. This was especially disappointing given that I had previously shared with Raghuvendra an incident involving my mother, where she had lent a substantial amount of money to my uncle and never got it back. After my father's passing, that money could have been our safety net, but it was lost to someone we trusted.

Raghuvendra was frustrated because he felt I wasn't learning from past mistakes, whether they were my own or others'. He pointed out that it's a poor attitude to wait for something bad to happen before learning the lessons. I understood his point, and I felt so foolish and mad at myself. I felt like a fool, but by then, it was too late. Sometimes, I wonder why I keep making these mistakes that leave me feeling disappointed in myself.

During this period, Raghuvendra and I went through some difficult days, ones that revealed my own unconscious habits and behaviour. At first, I thought they were minor, nothing to worry about. But slowly, as tensions built up, they became cracks in our relationship. Raghuvendra, sleep-deprived and increasingly frustrated, tried his best to handle it, yet his struggle seeped into me, stirring a sense of guilt I couldn't ignore. I knew that I needed to change, that I couldn't rely on the hope that everything would magically fix itself.

I had a two-day training scheduled with UNICEF in Delhi—a rare, inspiring opportunity where I met activists from around the world. But after missing my return flight to Varanasi, I was left stranded and discouraged. Raghuvendra stayed on the line to comfort me, only to be caught off guard when I quickly put him on hold for another call from my colleague. I didn't even think to explain; it was an unconscious move, one that stung him deeply. We'd already had misunderstandings before the flight, and this was the last straw. I could feel the sadness pooling inside me, breaking through the thin walls of composure as I sat alone in the crowded terminal, tears silently spilling over.

As I boarded the plane, my mind spiralled into dark questions. What if this is our future? What if our love, beautiful and alive, turned sour and crumbled like so many others? Relationships don't collapse overnight; they wither slowly, worn down by overlooked wounds, unmet needs, and missed moments of understanding. Long-distance only sharpens these edges, adding distance to every misstep. And I knew that even once we lived together, new hurdles would appear, new habits to harmonise. I dreaded the idea of growing resentful, of letting petty grievances steal our joy.

Sitting on the plane, I made a vow to myself. I had to change, to actively work on my own behaviour rather than letting my unconscious habits sabotage us. It was easy to overlook my part, to assume I'd adjust when the time came. But it was time to see myself with honesty. I began to look back at our fights, our misunderstandings, every little hurt. And as I pieced together each moment, a pattern emerged: I had been acting impulsively, thoughtlessly, hurting him without even realising it. I was repeating mistakes and expecting forgiveness without really growing.

Raghuvendra, meanwhile, often handled me with a gentle firmness, explaining what went wrong with a patience that now felt humbling. I had resisted it, but now I could see that he was trying to help, to nurture our bond in a way I hadn't appreciated. He believed in our potential, in our capacity to grow together, and so did I. But it was clear—I couldn't just rely on him to show the way. I needed to bring my own growth into our relationship.

In a quiet moment, I told him I was committed to changing, and to my relief, he promised to walk beside me on this journey. Raghuvendra, too, shared his own realisations. With raw honesty, he admitted he'd sometimes focused too much on my faults, letting frustration cloud his view of everything else I offered. He apologised, showing a rare vulnerability, and told me how much he admired my recent efforts, how grateful he was to be with me.

In that moment, I felt hope—a calm, steady belief that we could face whatever life brought us, as long as we stayed committed, as long as love and understanding guided us.

13. Unperturbed

As a society, we are disturbingly comfortable objectifying women, listening to songs that portray them as mere recipients of gifts, and even empowered women sing and dance to these tunes.

Raghuvendra:

On **July 05**, Shweta shared a significant yet bittersweet milestone in her career. One of six newly recruited staff from the NGO's Program Coordinator team in Jaunpur, she was now being reassigned to different districts. Her new posting was in Shrawasti, a region with a literacy rate of just 47%. For the past six months, Shweta had worked as part of a collaborative team of Program Coordinators and specialists in Jaunpur, surrounded by colleagues who shared her mission and eased the demands of their work. Now, with minimal preparation, she was tasked with independently overseeing the NGO's Program Supervisor role for the entire district. The weight of responsibility was compounded by the prospect of relocating to a small, unfamiliar town, adding an edge to her mounting stress.

I recall the gravity of our conversations about her new role and how her time in Jaunpur had been spent supporting underprivileged students, bridging the digital divide for both young and elderly populations. Her responsibilities ranged from coordinating program activities and maintaining data quality to documenting progress and building community awareness of the NGO's mission. She was a linchpin in the effort to motivate parents to enrol their children and inspire students to commit to their education. Her fieldwork exposed her to harsh realities—the struggles faced by young children forced into labour, the trauma of young girls facing harassment within their own homes, and the disturbing prevalence of coercion, begging, and theft among children manipulated by local gangs.

Her experiences had stripped away any lingering naivete about life in these regions; her anger and frustration were natural responses to witnessing violence and exploitation day after day, both in media as well as in real life. The prospect of relocating alone as a woman to a remote town stirred understandable fears in her, fears shared by countless women who face similar challenges.

As a man, I am reminded of the day-to-day struggles' women confront. It's likely we've all observed a girl walking quickly down the street, eyes lowered to avoid unwanted attention, hurrying home before dark, or forgoing simple needs like water for lack of safe, clean restrooms. While men often take basic needs for granted, women face countless barriers in their daily routines. These difficulties reflect deeply rooted issues within our families, our social structures, and our policymakers' priorities. Are we prepared to admit that we have failed, as a society, to create a safe and inclusive world for half of our population?

Every time a particularly horrific crime against women makes national headlines, outrage follows, and protests erupt. But what about the silent tragedies that never make it to the news? Why do crimes in big cities ignite national fury while similar incidents in small towns or rural areas go unnoticed? And why do so many public demonstrations of outrage seem fuelled by political ambitions rather than genuine concern for change? If our anger were truly focused on justice, wouldn't the public outcry hold politicians and officials accused of sexual harassment accountable? When even those tasked with upholding the law exploit their power, whom should we trust?

This failure does not start with governance alone; it begins at home. Why are so many young girls encouraged to prioritise appearance over ambition, or marriage over independence? Why do some parents still emphasise finding a "well-settled" man for their daughters, while many young women accept the idea of finding a financially stable partner rather than becoming financially independent themselves? Our societal comfort with objectifying women is disturbingly evident, whether it's in popular media or in the ways we unconsciously perpetuate these norms. Even so-called "honour" often revolves around a woman's sexual purity, leading to practices like honour killings or viewing a rape survivor as someone who has lost her dignity. In recent years, there have been cases where women were not only raped but brutally murdered; ironically, public outrage often centred on the assault, while the loss of life was barely mourned. What a tragic society we have fostered, where a woman's worth is reduced to her "purity" rather than her life.

Consider the representation of women in advertising. Why must they appear semi-nude to sell a product, whether it's lipstick or a car? For too long, women have been treated as objects of consumption, fantasies for male pleasure. In recent times, some women, under the guise of empowerment, have embraced forms of expression that might serve to reinforce rather than counter these objectifications. While the freedom to dress as one wishes is a fundamental right, is it truly empowering to make it the centrepiece of liberation? These are difficult questions to ask but dismissing them without reflection is a disservice.

So why haven't these marches, protests, and laws managed to curb issues like harassment and assault? Perhaps it's because we've become desensitised to the suffering around us, accepting discrimination and injustice as inevitable. Culprits are often well aware of the punishment they might face, yet this knowledge alone is insufficient to prevent crime. Real deterrence will come only when we, as a society, confront the underlying issues, beginning with our attitudes at home.

While building toilets for girls in government schools after decades of independence was an achievement, we must recognize that these steps are inadequate. Now, more than ever, it's time for a shift in mindset, a deep and collective introspection, and a commitment to setting our priorities right for a more just and safe future.

I was reminded that Shweta and I need to find a way to build a life together, one that allows us to spend time with each other and our families. Over the past year, Shweta and I have had many detailed conversations about life and work. Like any other couples, we both value flexibility in our schedules and don't want any limits on our financial growth. But we have witnessed the complexities faced by modern day couples where both genders have their personal aspirations and goals. The competitive job market further complicates the situation, often forcing couples to have years of long-distance relationships even after marriage. When we first started talking, Shweta was preparing for exams to secure a government job, and we had planned that she could join me in Germany for some time before we both moved back to India. But when she got the job in Uttar Pradesh, we were both happy and concerned.

The idea of being stuck in a job in a place with limited opportunities for the other partner was troubling. We've seen too many couples living in different cities, only meeting during festivals, with children growing up without a father's daily presence—it's a sad reality. I even tried applying for jobs in Uttar Pradesh to stay close to my ageing parents but had no luck. Small towns and cities have limited opportunities for both high-skilled and low-skilled workforces, and one of the highest urban migration rates in India. While the state has seen some improvements over the last few years, it's still far from ideal.

Despite understanding these challenges, I was worried that Shweta might feel pressured to quit her job to be with me. But to my surprise, she admitted that while security is good, growth demands discomfort. She recognized that although regular jobs offer security and have less risks, being self-employed offers growth and freedom. So, she had already decided to take on the challenge of becoming a health and wellness coach alongside her job. There will be struggles and a lot of learning involved, but she's willing to do whatever it takes, and I will be there to support her every step of the way. Above all, she wants to prioritise time with family and me and be her own boss.

It's a blessing to find someone so courageous and deeply in love with you. Never in my life had I imagined that we would trust each other's strength so completely. We don't know what the future holds, but if we don't ignore opportunities, we can start working toward better ones. Saying no is just the beginning of the universe opening doors for us.

One day, Shweta had a scheduled meeting with the Superintendent of Police (SP) regarding her work for the NGO. It was her first time directly interacting with senior administrative officers, and she felt proud to work alongside them. In UP and Bihar, administrative officer garners huge respect, and her excitement to have in person meetings was all associated with societal trends. She dressed elegantly in a full-sleeved Indian kurti with a white dupatta and the jutti I had gifted her, embodying a young, charming professional. I often advise her on maintaining confidence and a polished appearance at her workplace. I know how judgemental people can be at the workplace, they judge you with your dressing sense, position, salary and even social status. As a woman working alone in a small town, I believe she has to maintain a strong aura to prevent people from taking her lightly. While I used to think my advice might be overwhelming, she once reassured me, saying she genuinely loves it, calling me her "Mi_Professor."

Shweta talks very fast and gets nervous easily, which might make her seem underconfident. In the police department, where hierarchy and respect are based on how boldly you present yourself, it would be challenging for her to be fully respected if she doesn't make a great first impression. That's what was on my mind, though I don't know if it's true. She worshipped, took her bag, and started walking towards the office. I was on the phone with her, listening to the city's hustle and bustle in the background. She waited for almost half an hour before meeting.

It was already past 11:30 PM in Sweden, and I was about to sleep. I reminded her not to stress, to embrace the experience, stay calm, and breathe deeply when feeling nervous. I encouraged her to speak calmly and not rush, as people will listen attentively when you speak with power. After exchanging goodnight wishes, I slept.

I reminded her through text to listen to the audiobook I sent her last night, "COPYCAT MARKETING 101" by Burke Hedges. My friend Faisal suggested this book, and I found it eye-opening. I had been struggling to find a great mentor whose strategy I could emulate. Coming from a small town in Uttar Pradesh with limited role models, I struggled to grow beyond conventional thoughts and ideas of life. After living in different places and interacting with people from various walks of life, I've come to realise that we all have untapped potential waiting to be discovered. This book helped me understand the value of following the right success model. Knowing that Shweta had faced similar challenges in her career due to a lack of role models, I thought it would be a great read for her too. Shweta agreed and said she would listen to the audiobook.

Shweta:

As I was about to reach the office, with a confident aura I asked a passenger beside me in the taxi for the address of the Superintendent of Police (SP) office. The man kindly guided me, mentioning that it would be on the way, and even asked the driver to drop me off there. His respectful tone made me realise I was on the right path to present myself. When I arrived at the office, I made my way to the third floor and called the nodal officer, the District Superintendent of Police (DSP.) She called me into her office.

I was warmly welcomed by Mohini, the DSP. Her being female helped me feel more comfortable. In the police department, hierarchy is strictly maintained, and her seniority earned her respect from everyone, which I think enabled her to help me in every possible way.

Next, I was to meet the SP. I had already prepared myself for this, keeping Raghuvendra's reminder in mind to speak slowly, thoroughly, and calmly. I followed everything, and it worked like magic.

The DSP was genuinely impressed with my work at the NGO and extended an invitation for dinner, which I gladly accepted. That evening, I waited at our reserved table, and she arrived with her adorable twin children. Over dinner, we shared a warm conversation, discussing my work and experiences in the district. By the end, she assured me, saying, "If you ever face any issues here, feel free to reach out. I'm always here for you."

This experience left me feeling truly grateful; she felt like my cheerleader, making me appreciate my work even more. Reflecting on the journey, I realise how challenging it was initially, arriving with no support and still managing to secure proper accommodation, handling a heavy workload, and gathering data. My first days were filled with constant running around; I would often work late into the night just to ensure every report was accurate and every activity accounted for. The NGO's funding limitations meant juggling resources and managing a team with minimal supplies, which sometimes made me feel like I was holding things together with sheer willpower.

Beyond the logistics, understanding and gaining the trust of local communities was a big hurdle. Many were sceptical of yet another organisation promising change, and building relationships required patience and genuine intent, often involving long conversations to address their doubts. At times, I felt overwhelmed by the emotional weight of the poverty, abuse, and child labour I witnessed firsthand. My data science course proved invaluable, helping me manage data effectively under pressure. And

Raghuvendra's support—even in subtle ways—was a tremendous help. Isn't it magical knowing someone is there for you, no matter what? It gives such emotional strength. They say love makes you powerful, and now, I truly understand why.

Life seemed to be moving smoothly until the news of my grandmother's hospitalisation disrupted everything. She was critically ill, admitted to the ICU, and struggling with a recurring respiratory infection that had intensified over the past week. Just weeks before, she'd undergone surgery to remove a benign tumour from her stomach—a challenging recovery for someone over eighty. I felt a deep urge to be by her side. She had been a window into my father's life, sharing stories from his childhood and youth, memories my mother never could bear to recount without becoming too emotional. Those stories had always brought a sense of closeness to him, and now, more than ever, I needed to be near her.

I took leave from work and caught a bus the next morning at ten, heading first to Bahraich and then transferring to Lucknow. When we're at our lowest, we find ourselves drawn to the people we love, not necessarily because they can share in our pain, but because their presence offers a small escape, a momentary balm to our sorrows.

By the time I reached Lucknow, it was already quite late. Exhausted, I stayed at my uncle's apartment—he worked as a station master—and went straight to bed, my only focus on scrolling through my phone. In my tiredness, I forgot to wish Raghuvendra goodnight, though it didn't even cross my mind then. The next morning, I waited to hear from him, but it turned out he had gone to sleep early the previous night. Without realising I'd done the same, I started feeling irritated, annoyed he hadn't informed me about his schedule.

Throughout the day, as I juggled family obligations and my time with Raghuvendra grew limited, minor misunderstandings began piling up. My late responses to his messages, only made worse by my busy surroundings, seemed to add fuel to the fire. I could feel a distance creeping in, an unspoken tension. Soon, we were both tiptoeing around each other's words, careful but also slightly resentful. The leave I'd taken was short, so after only two days, I had to return. I let Raghuvendra know I was on the bus, only for him to realise I hadn't even mentioned when I was planning to leave in the first place.

Once I arrived home, I dove back into pending work, attempting to catch up after the past few chaotic days. Raghuvendra was also set to go on a trip that evening, his time overlapping with my night. Normally, our time zones were manageable, with only a four-and-a-half-hour difference, even after he'd moved from Germany to Sweden. But that night, as I was finally ready for a deep sleep, Raghuvendra messaged, "Stop acting like everything is normal." He was right. Things weren't normal between us.

Yet, as exhausted as I was, I didn't think it was the moment to discuss our problems. Our conversation escalated quickly, and before I knew it, I'd said things in a harsh tone I hadn't intended. I knew it must have hurt him, especially since my communication had been all over the place. But sometimes, I felt Raghuvendra could be too particular, holding onto small issues and discussing them at length until I felt low and a bit diminished. As much as I knew it was my fault this time, a part of me wished he'd let go of these details that gnawed away at my confidence.

The next day, we both came to the conclusion that maybe a short break was needed—a week to clear our minds and reset. The days that followed were long and hollow. Without Raghuvendra, everything felt dulled, like life had lost some of its colour. I stopped picking up my phone to call anyone, though I constantly checked his last-seen status. We shared a group chat where we exchanged a message or two, but they were few and far between. Each day dragged on, a slow, empty stretch, reminding me just how deeply he filled my world, even when things felt off.

On the first day of our break, I felt completely drained. Every little issue seemed monumental; my mind weighed down by an exhaustion that reached my bones. Even the smallest tasks seemed to look like insurmountable mountains. By the second day, though, I knew I didn't want this silence, this gap between us, to stretch on any longer. I needed to find a solution—to break through whatever barrier had come between us and let it melt away. I resolved to end this "no-talk" phase before it grew roots.

On the third day, I began looking inward, questioning myself and peeling back the layers to find the root of the issue. Sitting with a notebook, I asked myself, "What am I bringing into this relationship?" I needed to understand where I could improve, where I could let go, and where my own insecurities were stirring up conflict. The more I reflected, the more I understood that adjustments are part of the rhythm of any relationship. There are moments when both partners need to meet each other halfway, but there are also times when one has to carry the weight of resolution. That's the nature of balance. To make a relationship remarkable, I realised, you need to be willing to put in remarkable effort.

As I reflected, memories of Raghuvendra's quiet acts of love came rushing back. So many times, he had dropped habits or behaviours I casually mentioned I didn't like, no explanations asked, simply because he respected my feelings. And yet, I often struggled to make similar changes for him. I recalled moments when my actions might have triggered insecurities in him, times I hadn't been fully mindful, and he had still accepted me without a single complaint. He always made me feel like a priority, no matter how busy or far away he was. In that moment, gratitude overwhelmed me, a deep, humbling realisation of how blessed I was to have him in my life.

After those seven days—a stretch that had felt like an eternity—our break finally came to an end. When I shared my insights with Raghuvendra, he seemed genuinely satisfied, a relief that made me feel all the hardship and introspection of the past week had not been in vain.

Just as life seemed to settle, a wave of sadness swept over me with news that my grandmother had passed away. Her battle had ended in respiratory failure after months of struggling, and though I felt deep sadness, there was a peace in knowing she was no longer suffering. My grandmother had always been a pillar of strength, someone who had managed our home and farmland tirelessly. Losing her felt like time itself had taken something precious, a reminder that life, in its quiet way, moves us all forward. She wouldn't be there to see me get married, a thought that weighed on my heart, but I knew her blessings would be there, guiding me from beyond.

14. The Failed Plan

All relationships are built on expectations, whether obvious or subtle.

Raghuvendra:

It took us months to truly accept and appreciate each other. From being unsure if we even liked one another, to becoming emotionally attached, we had come a long way. Along the way, we also realised something else expectations had quietly crept into our relationship. I had often wondered why people advised expecting nothing from others. To me, it never made sense. If I couldn't expect love, care, and attention from my partner, what was there to emotionally bond with her over? Shweta had already communicated her expectations early on, starting with something as simple as her birthday. But she had learned to hold back her emotions, protecting herself from my fluctuating mental state.

Looking back, the journey from our first meeting to now has taught us something vital: all relationships are built on expectations, whether obvious or subtle. And without effective communication and mutual effort, those expectations often become the root cause of a relationship's downfall.

Surprisingly, after every argument, we grew stronger as a couple. We were evolving, working on ourselves and towards common goals. In our casual conversations, we started visualising our wedding day. One day, I asked Shweta what she expected from the wedding day. She admitted that, until recently, she had dreamed of a grand celebration. But after attending the lavish wedding of a childhood friend, she realised it was more about showing off than embracing the sacredness of marriage. The rituals felt rushed, the photographer hovered over the couple like an unwanted shadow, and people seemed more focused on the food than the ceremony. It was a lot of waste—plastic, money, and, most importantly, meaning.

I, on the other hand, had always envisioned a simple wedding. No pomp and show, just an intimate, eco-friendly ceremony. I wanted to use biodegradable materials for decor and cutlery, donate fruit trees to mark the occasion, and even organise a collective event for underprivileged couples. When I shared these ideas with Shweta, she embraced them wholeheartedly. She agreed that a simple wedding would be perfect. "I just want you," she said, smiling, "because marriage is just the beginning, and now that we've accepted each other, any tradition will work for me." Her words made me feel loved and understood.

But when I shared these thoughts with my dad, he thought I was crazy. My brother understood my perspective, but he was hesitant to challenge our father. After a deeper conversation, my father explained his concerns. We live in a society that clung to its norms, and deviating from them often led to gossip and judgement. "I understand your ideas," he said, "and I appreciate them. But we have to live in this society, and following its customs is a way to live gracefully."

Though my parents are elderly and could easily be mislabelled as holding old-fashioned views, they are surprisingly open to change. Even when they find it difficult to take action themselves, they always ensure that we feel heard. They make a point of explaining their perspectives rather than imposing them. It's their way of balancing tradition with the evolving values of our generation—by not standing in the way, but rather by encouraging us to make thoughtful decisions, even when those decisions challenge societal norms. He had already firmly rejected the idea of dowry, a practice deeply ingrained in our region. Shweta's family felt relieved knowing we truly meant what we said about rejecting dowry.

Dowry and extravagant weddings are huge issues in India. You'd be surprised to know that one of my friends had his wedding cancelled because he refused to accept any dowry or gifts. The girl's family thought something must be wrong with him; otherwise, why would an eligible man, who could easily demand a large dowry, turn it down? It's absurd how both sides of a family perpetuate this outdated practice. And as for grand weddings, Indian parents often spend a significant portion of their savings on their children's weddings. Some even sell property, take loans, or mortgage gold to make the event as lavish as possible, with a vast array of food, entertainment, ornaments, and gifts—not just for close family members, but even for distant relatives. If they don't, society might label them stingy or antisocial.

I understood my father's dilemma. It was a harsh realisation of how deeply societal norms are entrenched, making it nearly impossible to break free. Still, I was determined to stand by my values. I decided to talk to

Shweta's mom, but first, I asked her to initiate the conversation. When she broached the topic with her, her response was similar. She was okay with our desire for a simple wedding, but, as she put it, "What will society say?
"

It hit us hard—people were willing to suffer, complain, and yet still continue these traditions, all for the sake of what society might think. We realised that a society which doesn't question or update its customs, traditions, and values can become stagnant and even detrimental. It became clear to us that meaningful change doesn't happen overnight. Maybe we have to start with baby steps, challenging outdated norms in small, personal ways before we learn how to make the larger disruptions necessary for broader change.

It's about balance—standing up for what we believe in without completely alienating those around us, especially those who are tied to these long-standing practices. Slowly but surely, as more people begin to question and take these smaller steps, society can evolve.

We might not be able to change everything immediately, but we can start with our own lives and hope to inspire others along the way. That realisation gave us a sense of purpose, knowing that even our seemingly small decision to date each other in an arranged marriage could ripple outwards and create a better future. Perhaps, our story could lead parents, men, and women alike to reflect on their own lives—comprehend the depth of human connection—and bring meaningful changes to their thought process, customs, and the way they perceive relationships.

It's time to stop seeing society as the sole regulatory element in love and marriage. Instead, relationships should be built on mutual respect, trust, and personal values, not on what others expect or demand. If Raghvendra and Shweta's journey can prompt even a few people to question outdated traditions and put the essence of partnership above societal pressures, then maybe we are already making the change we once thought impossible.

Glossary

Aalo paratha - potato pancake.

Aarti - a Hindu/Sanatani ritual employed in worship.

Abeer/gulal - brightly coloured powder.

Agua - a trusted mutual connection who acts as a facilitator between the two families.

Bade Achhe Lagte Hain - a daily soap aired in India.

Bahu - daughter-in-law.

Banarasi saree - a traditional silk saree from Varanasi, known for its rich fabric, intricate designs, and luxurious gold or silver Zari work.

Bhindi bhujia - spiced okra fry.

Bhujia - pan-fried and steamed vegetable.

Bhutta - fresh maize roasted over a bonfire.

Bindi- a coloured dot or a sticker worn on the centre of the forehead, originally by Hindus, Jains and Buddhists from the Indian subcontinent.

Biryani - a dish originally from South Asia consisting of rice with meat, fish, or vegetables and various spices.

Bua - dad's sister.

Chana - black chickpea.

Chakhna - some snacks which are often served to complement alcoholic beverages

Chawal - rice.

Chhath - an ancient Sanatani Vedic festival dedicated to the Sun God (Surya) and his wife Usha, primarily celebrated in the Indian states of Bihar, Jharkhand, Uttar Pradesh, and the Terai region of Nepal.

Chikankari kurta - a garment featuring chikankari, a traditional embroidery style from Lucknow, India.

Chokha - mashed vegetable side dish served with Litti.

Chunari - a special bridal dupatta/long scarf.

Churis - a kind of thin colourful glass bangles worn by females in India and its neighbouring countries.

Chutney – a thick, flavourful sauce of Indian origin, typically made from a variety of ingredients such as coriander leaves, mint, coconut, lemon, chilies, mango, tomatoes, tamarind, salt, sugar, or a combination of these. It is commonly used as a condiment to enhance the flavour of dishes.

Daal - pulses, but often referred to soup made from Pulses.

Darshan - offering prayers

Dhaba - a roadside café or food stall.

Dupatta - a long shawl-like scarf traditionally worn by women in India.

Fire paan - made by placing a combustible substance over betel nut leaves which is then lighted before putting in the mouth.

Ghee tadka - tempering with clarified butter.

Gulab-jal - rose water.

Gupteshwor Mahadev Cave - cave beneath the ground.

Ghum-ne Ch(a)-lay - let's go travelling.

Hanuman Chalisa- prayer.

Hanuman ji- the Hindu monkey god of wisdom and power.

Holi- the vibrant and deeply significant Hindu festival known as the Festival of Colours, Love, and Spring.

Holika Dahan- a bonfire is lit to symbolise the victory of good over evil.

Jalebis - deep-fried intersecting ring-shaped desserts made using fermented refined flour which are then soaked in sugar syrup.

Kajal - a black cosmetic used around the eyes in South Asia.

Kalpa - a very long period of time in Hindu and Buddhist cosmology, usually in billions of years.

Kangan - a kind of bangle, broader than usual churis/bangles for the wrist worn by women.

Karma - the force generated by a person's actions in Hinduism and Buddhism, believed to determine future life experiences.

Khasti Mahachaitya - great stupa of the dew drops.

Kundru - ivy gourd.

Kurtis - short kurta, referred to as kurti, the attire of females.

Laphing - a spicy cold noodle dish garnished with chilli oil, soy sauce, and vinegar.

Litti - a traditional dish from Bihar, UP and Jharkhand states of made from spiced black gram powder stuffed in balls made from whole wheat flour cooked over open flame, mainly coal/charcoal.

Maa- mother

Maang tikka - a forehead ornament for females.

Machhapuchhre - "Fishtail," refers to the fish-tail like shape of its twin summits.

Mahendra cave - a popular natural limestone cave located near Pokhara, Nepal.

Malpua - a deep-fried dessert made with refined flour dough and sugar.

Masala- Spice.

Momos- Indian/ Nepali dumplings

Paan – a traditional Indian treat made with a betel leaf filled with chopped areca nut, slaked lime, and a variety of ingredients such as spices and dried fruits.

Pakoras - veggies dipped in spiced chickpea flour and deep-fried.

Palak ka aachar - spinach pickle.

Papad - a thin roasted pancake, usually made from legume flour.

Patale Chango- Underworld's Waterfall.

Panchmukhi- five headed

Paneer paratha - cottage cheese pancake.

Persian polao (Pulaf) - a traditional rice dish from Persia (modern-day Iran) that involves cooking rice with various spices, meat, vegetables, or dried fruits.

Pyaj paratha - onion pancake.

Rawa - suji (semolina).

Roka - a ritual promising that the families will not seek other partners for their child.

Roti - Indian flat bread.

Sabji - vegetables or vegetable curries.
Samosas - triangular pastry with a savoury filling, mostly vegetables or spiced potatoes, deep-fried in oil.

Saraswati Puja- a Hindu festival dedicated to the goddess of wisdom and education, Saraswati.

Saree - a long piece of cloth worn by women, particularly in the Indian subcontinent, draped around the body.

Sarnath - a small town on the outskirts of the city Varanasi.

Shivaratri - the day when Lord Shiva and Goddess Parvati were married.

Thakali thali - a traditional meal from the Thakali community in Nepal, known for its variety and balanced flavours.

Thangkas - a form of Buddhist art used in temples and monasteries.

Thukpa - a Tibetan-style noodle soup with vegetables.

Varanasi - an ancient holy city in Uttar Pradesh, India

Priyanka Kumari and Dr. Chandan Kumar Gautam are a loving husband-and-wife duo, united by their passion for creating a positive impact on society and the environment. Together, they lead Harmony in Nourishment (HiNt), a health and wellness initiative, where they also serve as wellness coaches, promoting balanced living and holistic well-being. Priyanka, a forensic expert in India, has authored a research article and contributed to an upcoming academic book. Dr. Gautam, a plant biologist in the USA, has published several scientific papers in prestigious journals.

This novel marks their first venture into fiction writing, a heartfelt collaboration that combines their creativity and shared vision.